Vale has always taken his job as an assassin seriously, which means killing his targets without asking questions and keeping his mouth shut. When he finds a picture of an old target of his in the hotel room of a man he just disposed of, he knows something fishy is happening. Luckily for him, his target doesn't have to stay dead.

Cyril is surprised when his boyfriend asks him to reanimate his latest target, because that's not how his job usually works. He'd do anything for Vale, though, so he does it, only to find himself pulled into a mess he has nothing to do with for once.

Some people have more money than sense, and Peter West is one of those people. He wants Vale killed so he can't tell anyone that he had his father killed, which makes Vale the prey instead of the predator. More importantly, it puts Cyril in danger, something Vale can't accept.

He'll have to get extra friendly with death this time around.

Friendly With Death
Copyright © 2024 Catherine Lievens
ISBN: 978-1-4874-4175-3
Cover art by Angela Waters

Published by eXtasy Books Inc

Look for us online at:
www.eXtasybooks.com

FRIENDLY WITH DEATH
NOT QUITE DEAD 2

BY

CATHERINE LIEVENS

CHAPTER ONE

The first thing Vale saw when he opened his eyes was bones.

Oscar was a heavy weight on Vale's chest. Just a few weeks ago, Vale would've jumped, maybe screamed a little at the sight. Now, he sighed and reached out to scratch the top of the skull that made up Oscar's body.

Oscar made the weird purring sound he always made when he was happy. He wasn't a cat, so Vale had no idea why or how he made it, but thinking too hard about it gave him the creeps, so he stopped. He didn't understand Oscar or how Cyril had made him, and he didn't care. It was none of his business.

Even though the weird bone octopus was curled up on top of him.

Vale's life had become even weirder than before. He couldn't regret that when it had brought him Cyril, but sometimes he wondered how he'd managed to get involved. He'd gone from having a fairly normal and boring life to living with a necromancer and his pet.

"Where's Cyril?" Vale asked.

He doubted Cyril had gone very far. His boyfriend rarely left the apartment except for jobs, preferring the comfort of his home to going out there in the world and having to deal with people. Apparently, he'd much rather deal with dead people than with alive ones, which made his everyday life slightly complicated. It wasn't like Cyril was a hermit or anything like that, but he was a little weird, and people tended to give him a wide berth when they found out he was a necromancer.

Vale supposed that people would do the same to him if they knew he was a professional killer. It was a good thing he never told anyone. Cyril, on the other hand, couldn't exactly hide what he was.

But Cyril wasn't alone anymore. He had Vale and Russell and, in a way, Rachel. He'd never met her, but he would eventually.

Oscar poked at Vale's cheek with one of his weird bone tentacles. Vale realized he'd stopped scratching him, so he started again, lightly glaring at the pet. Sometimes he still tried making sense of his life and of Oscar, but he'd realized soon after getting with Cyril that his life didn't have to make sense for him to be happy. He had a necromancer boyfriend and a weird pet. It didn't matter how it worked or how he'd obtained it.

He hesitated before gingerly wrapping his hands around Oscar's body. That was still really fucking weird, too. To pick Oscar up, Vale had to pick up his skull body, which creeped him out even though he'd killed dozens of people. Usually, when he killed, his targets weren't bony. He didn't often have to deal with skeletons, let alone skeletons that a necromancer had reanimated.

Oscar wrapped his tentacles around Vale's arms as if trying to cling to him. Knowing him, that was what he was doing. He loved cuddles, and while he got plenty from Cyril, for some reason, he'd gotten attached to Vale since pretty much the day they'd met. If Vale hadn't known better, he would have thought that Oscar was doing it on purpose because he knew that Vale was weirded out.

Actually, there might be something there. Oscar's body was made with a human skull. Vale still wasn't entirely sure how Cyril's ability worked, but he wouldn't be surprised if, by using a human skull, Cyril had given Oscar human traits. Maybe Oscar was teasing. Maybe the person the skull had belonged to had been playful and friendly.

Vale sat up and raised Oscar to his face. He stared at the empty eye sockets of Oscar's body, shuddered, and put him down on the bed. None of this mattered. Knowing whether or not Oscar had a human personality wouldn't change the fact that he was freaking creepy and half in love with Vale. Vale just had to get used to having him around.

Luckily for him, that came with a cute boyfriend.

Vale got out of bed and went in search of his man, stopping in the bathroom before heading to the kitchen. He could smell coffee and toast, so he knew that Cyril wasn't far.

Just like he'd expected, Vale found his boyfriend in the window seat. Cyril's hands were wrapped around a mug that had to be full of tea rather than coffee. Cyril made coffee in the morning for Vale but seldom drank it, preferring tea and herbal mixtures that smelled foul. He'd tried to convince Vale to drink them a few times, but Vale wouldn't even smell them, let alone let them anywhere near his mouth. Coffee, though, he could do, and he was grateful that Cyril always thought of him when he was the first to wake up in the morning.

Vale stopped next to Cyril and leaned down to kiss the top of his head. Cyril turned, looking sleepy but happy, and smiled at him. "I thought you'd sleep longer," he said.

"I can go back to bed if you want me to." Vale grinned. "In fact, you could come back to bed with me."

Cyril's cheeks flushed. From what he'd told Vale, he hadn't had many people in his life beyond his mother. People didn't understand what being a necromancer meant, and even when they did, they were usually wary of him. It was ridiculous, but human beings usually were. Vale didn't care that his boyfriend could reanimate the dead. He only cared that Cyril was sweet, gentle, and caring.

He would give the shirt off his back to anyone just because they asked for it, even if they didn't need it. He took a lot of jobs pro bono because he could and because he wanted to help. His heart hurt for the people he helped because they'd lost someone important to them, and he did everything he could to make the experience easier. Cyril wasn't perfect, but he was as perfect as they came, and Vale would always be grateful and stunned that Cyril had chosen him of all people.

"I made you coffee," Cyril offered.

"I can tell. Thank you. You didn't have to."

Cyril shrugged. "I wanted to."

Vale kissed him again just because he could. "I don't know what I'd do without you."

"I think you'd survive just fine."

"Survive, probably, but would I want to? I don't think so. You brighten my life, Cyril. If you weren't in it, it would become rather dull and dark."

The flush on Cyril's cheeks darkened. Vale grinned at him, pleased to get that reaction from his boyfriend. Cyril deserved to be loved and cared for. He'd been alone for way too long, but he wasn't anymore. Now he had Vale, and Vale would ensure that Cyril never felt alone again.

Cyril knew that his cheeks were flushed. He wasn't embarrassed by what Vale had said, but he still wasn't fully used to someone flirting with him. Most of the time, he had no idea how to react. Sometimes he felt like he should wink, but at the same time, that would make him feel like a creep, and he'd rather not. Just staring at Vale with hearts in his eyes also felt ridiculous, but it wasn't like Cyril could *not* say anything. Vale flirted with him to get a reaction out of him, right? That meant that Cyril had to react.

But how?

Cyril settled on smiling. He supposed that if everything else failed, a nice smile would help. Besides, it wasn't like Vale would judge him, even if he was ridiculous. For some reason, Vale wanted Cyril just the way he was. Cyril still wasn't entirely sure why that was, but he'd stopped trying to find a reason behind all of this. It didn't matter. The only thing that did was that Vale had fallen for Cyril and wanted him in his life. Cyril didn't have to analyze why. He just had to enjoy his first real relationship.

And hopefully, his last.

He couldn't see himself with anyone but Vale, and it had nothing to do with the fact that until him, people tended to run the other way when they found out what Cyril did for a living. Most people didn't want anything to do with a guy who could reanimate the dead, even though Cyril tried to only do it for good reasons. If he could afford it, he wouldn't make people pay for what he did. He always felt guilty, like he was taking advantage of people during one of the worst periods of their lives, but he had to keep the lights on and eat, and unfortunately, that meant getting paid.

With Vale's help, he was starting to realize that maybe he actually deserved this. His ability came to him as naturally as breathing, but it was rare. Why shouldn't he use it? And why shouldn't he get paid to use it? Most of the people who contacted him could afford it. That was why they contacted him in the first place. The ones who couldn't, well, let's just say that Cyril could probably have been a millionaire by now if he got everyone to pay what most other necromancers would view as a good price.

But he didn't care about money. He never had. He just wanted to help people, and his ability meant that he could. That was all that mattered to him.

That, and the few people he cared about.

Vale's smile was fond and gentle as he leaned down to kiss

Cyril's cheek, and Cyril realized he hadn't answered Vale's offer to return to bed. His cheeks heated, but Vale was already moving away. He didn't look offended or angry. He never did, especially not when Cyril was involved, which was a new experience. Vale had infinite patience. Sometimes Cyril was afraid it would end, but so far, it hadn't. Of course, they'd only just gotten together. Things might change.

Cyril didn't think Vale would.

He got up from the window seat and stretched before joining Vale in the kitchen. Vale was sipping on coffee, glaring at Oscar, who was sitting on the kitchen counter.

"I don't think that's hygienic," Vale said. "I mean, technically, I know he's made of bones and that he doesn't eat or have any bodily functions, but still. Should he really sit where we prepare food?"

Cyril put down his mug and grabbed Oscar. "I'll try to teach him not to do it."

Vale snorted. "You can try to teach him, but I doubt he'll learn, or rather, he'll learn and ignore it. He does what he wants."

Cyril scratched the top of Oscar's head. "Yes, well. He was here before you."

"He's not going to be here for much longer if he doesn't learn the rules," Vale grumbled.

Cyril hugged Oscar against his chest and smiled. Both he and Oscar knew that Vale was joking. He would never dare kick Oscar out, and not just because he knew it would hurt Cyril. Vale actually liked Oscar, even though he would never admit it out loud.

Vale had never even said anything against Oscar beyond the first few times they'd met when Vale was shocked and a bit freaked out because he didn't understand what Oscar was. There wasn't an explanation. Cyril had cobbled Oscar together with a bunch of bones when he'd been lonely and yearning for a friend, and Oscar had been that for him ever since. Cyril had Vale now, but Oscar would always be his first friend, and he would always love him.

Hygienic or not.

Vale's phone vibrated. He snatched it up from the counter and stared at the screen for a moment, frowning. "Artemis emailed me," he explained as he slid his fingers on the screen.

Cyril swallowed. Cyril's job was hard for a lot of people to accept, but most people could never accept Vale's. He was a professional killer. It wasn't something Cyril had ever thought much about, even though, for his job, he often had to revive people who'd been killed by professionals. He usually only saw the result of their hits, but he'd never met one of them until Vale.

And now he shared a bed with one.

Cyril was a bit conflicted when it came to Vale's job. He supposed that he was used to death, so it didn't horrify him as it would most people, but it still made him uncomfortable. The thought of Vale killing people because he was paid to do so was weird. Cyril had asked him a lot of questions initially, and he'd been reassured when Vale had told him that he only took specific kinds of jobs. He didn't hurt innocent people, people who didn't deserve to die, or children. He trusted Artemis to select the right jobs for him, and knowing that had made Cyril feel better about all of it. It was still weird to think that Vale was killing people while Cyril reanimated them, but they made it work.

"She has a local job for me," Vale commented. "She says she would've sent it to Russell, but he's still out of town."

"What job?"

"It looks pretty straightforward. The guy works for a big company. It says here that he killed his former boss."

"Why isn't he in jail?"

Vale gave Cyril a fond look that was reserved for him.

"Most of the time, the police don't know how to do their job. Even if they try, and they don't always, it could have been anything. Maybe there wasn't enough proof, or maybe there was, but the guy was let go by a jury. Either way, the victim's son wants this guy dead because of what he did to his father."

"You're going to take the job?"

"I think so. I don't have to travel, and it seems pretty straightforward."

He hesitated and stared at Cyril for a moment. Cyril wondered what he was thinking.

"You know that I can fully retire if you're not comfortable with me doing this, right?" Vale offered. "I've been thinking about it, anyway. I can't continue killing people for the rest of my life, and frankly, I want to be able to focus on you. I just need to be able to pay the bills."

"I can pay the bills."

"I won't be a kept man. I appreciate your willingness to help me out, but I want to help, too."

Cyril got that. It didn't mean he had to like it. "You should take the job, and if you want to fully retire, I'll support you, but you don't have to do it just because you think it's what I want."

Vale put down his phone and grabbed Cyril's waist, pulling him close. Cyril didn't resist. He never did, not when it came to Vale.

Vale wrapped his arms around Cyril and looked down at him. "You say that I don't have to consider what you want when I make decisions about my life, but that's not how relationships work," Vale said gently. "I want you to have opinions and thoughts about things. I want to know what you'd be more comfortable with."

"I'd be more comfortable if you didn't go out there to kill people," Cyril admitted. "But I understand that it's not like you can just find another job. I don't expect you to give up your independence just because I don't agree with what you do."

"I'll tell Rachel that I'll take the job, but I'll also ask her to poke around and see what my next step could be. I don't have the faintest idea what I could do if I'm not a professional assassin, but it doesn't mean I'm not going to try to find out."

"For me?" Cyril asked, even though he knew it would be for him.

Vale kissed Cyril's forehead. "For you, I would do this and so much more. I don't need or want to be a professional killer. I do need and want you, though."

Cyril wasn't used to people telling him that, and he basked in the feeling. Whatever Vale decided, it didn't matter as long as he stayed in Cyril's life.

CHAPTER TWO

Vale was still thinking about his conversation with Cyril a few days later when he headed out on the job. He understood that not many people would be comfortable with what he did for a living, but a necromancer especially so. Cyril's job was to reanimate dead people, while Vale's was to kill them. Most people would be surprised to find out how well they worked together, but neither Cyril nor Vale were their jobs.

Still, knowing that Cyril was uncomfortable meant that Vale wanted to speed up his retirement. His job had only ever been a job for him, and he wouldn't miss it. He just wanted to find something else to do before actually retiring.

That was where things got complicated. It wasn't like he could just write up a resume and send it around. The only experience he had was in killing people, and he doubted most people would want to hire someone like him. Of course, he wasn't planning on going about this the normal way. He could never have a normal job in an office or in a store or anything like that. He didn't *want* that kind of job. He just needed to find something that paid well and that wouldn't take him away from Cyril.

He was still thinking about that as he walked into the hotel where he would find his target. He made his way upstairs to the room Artemis had given him the number of, snuck inside, and looked around. He could hear the shower, which was good because it meant that cleanup would be easier for the hotel staff. Vale tried to be considerate when he could.

He opened the bathroom door, stepped in, and got his gun

out. He needed to be sure that the man he was about to kill was the target, so he grabbed the shower curtain and pulled it to the side.

The man inside the shower turned. He opened his mouth, no doubt to scream, but Vale had recognized him from the picture Artemis had emailed him. He didn't give the man any time to raise the alarm. He shot him between the eyes, watched as his body crumpled down, and waited for a few seconds, just in case. He'd never had a target come back from the dead right after he'd killed them, but now that he was with Cyril, he never knew what to expect. He wouldn't be surprised if, one day, one of his targets just got up and yelled at him for killing them.

This guy didn't. He stayed down, the water turning pink as he bled. Vale turned it off, and for a moment, the silence was so loud it made him want to scream.

He was done. Hopefully, this would be his last job.

He went back to the hotel room, ready to go, but he stumbled on a pair of shoes that had been abandoned on the floor. He fell forward, swearing as he went, and bumped into the coffee table. A bunch of documents that had been on the table fluttered to the floor, and Vale would have ignored them if he hadn't recognized the guy in one of the pictures.

He crouched next to the fallen documents and picked up a picture. He was wearing gloves, so no one would find his fingerprints on the thing.

He stared at the face looking back at him. It took him a moment to realize he recognized the guy.

He'd killed him.

Vale had killed a lot of people in his career, but he remembered this one. He'd recognized the man as soon as Artemis had told him about the hit on him. John West had owned one of the biggest companies in the country, and through it, he'd done every unethical thing anyone could think.

Why did Vale's new target have a picture of one of his old targets?

Something strange was happening, and Vale didn't like it. He'd learned to listen to his instincts over the years, and they were never wrong. If he thought something was odd, then something was odd, which meant he needed more information. He doubted Artemis would have anything for him beyond what she'd already given him.

Vale glanced toward the bathroom. He knew how he could get more information, but he wasn't sure how happy Cyril would be to help him. He'd do it because that was what he did and because he was in love with Vale, but Vale hated feeling like he was taking advantage of their relationship.

He looked back down at the picture of John West. He didn't have a choice. It was clear something was happening, and the dead guy might be the only way for him to find out what it was. If it was only for him, he might not have wanted to know, but he had Cyril to think about now. He had to protect him, and if anyone found out that he and Cyril were together, they would try to use him to get to Vale.

Vale had to know what was happening, and there was only one way for him to do that.

He took out his phone, quickly emailed Artemis, and pulled up Cyril's number. He couldn't believe what he was about to do, but it reminded him of the way he and Cyril had met. Vale hadn't asked Cyril to reanimate his targets then, but Cyril had because the families had paid him to do it. Now, it was Vale who would have to pay him to reanimate someone he killed.

Russell was going to find this hilarious when he found out about it.

Cyril smiled when his phone rang and he saw Vale's name on

the phone. He was probably calling to tell Cyril that he was done with the job and headed back home. He knew Cyril was always a bit anxious when he was out on jobs.

He answered with a smile. "Already done?"

"I am, actually, but I need you to come here and reanimate my target."

Cyril blinked and stared at the wall in front of the couch. "I'm sorry?"

Vale sighed. "You heard me. I need you to reanimate my target."

"Why? What happened?" Had Vale made a mistake? Did he kill the wrong person? It didn't sound like something he'd do. Besides, he was asking Cyril to reanimate his target, not someone he might have killed by mistake.

"There's something weird about this," Vale said. "And, of course, I didn't realize it until after I'd already killed the guy. I bumped into the coffee table and found a picture of one of my old targets. There's something fishy going on, and I need to know what it is, but my target is dead."

"Which is why you need me."

"I always need you, but yeah. If I want to know what's going on, I'm going to have to talk to the guy I just killed."

Cyril would do pretty much anything for Vale, so he was off the couch before Vale could stop talking. "I'll come."

"Thank you. I know this probably makes you uncomfortable, but I didn't know who else to call."

"I'm glad you called me. It's what I do."

"You don't usually reanimate my targets."

Cyril snorted. "Actually, I do. It's how we met."

"You think you're funny."

"I know I am, and Russell's going to find it hilarious when we tell him about it."

"Don't remind me. I really don't want to deal with him when he's like that."

13

"You'll tell him anyway." Mostly because Vale and Russell were friends, but also because if something weird was going on, Vale would want Russell's help. Even when he could do something on his own, Vale would rather work with Russell and Rachel.

Cyril loved that. He'd always worked alone, but then, most necromancers did. Some of them had assistants who took care of booking their appointments and things like that, but while Cyril had enough work to warrant having one of those, he'd always felt uncomfortable with the thought. It probably had a lot to do with the fact that most people would rather cross the road than cross paths with him, but he didn't think he would ever be able to trust someone like that. That was one of the reasons he'd been so happy when Vale had told him that he wanted to work with him. It wasn't the kind of work Vale was used to, so they were still trying to fit everything together, but at least Cyril hadn't had to learn how to work with a stranger.

For now. He doubted Vale would want to be his assistant for long if he retired. It would be a boring job for someone who was used to what Vale did so Cyril wouldn't blame him. He'd just enjoy their time together for as long as he could.

"Text me the address, and I'll be right there," he promised.

"I'll see you soon."

They hung up, and Cyril quickly got ready. Luckily his bag was packed because when he got a call for a job, he had to go as soon as possible, so he only had to say goodbye to Oscar and put on his jacket and his shoes. By then, his phone had already pinged with the address of the place where he was going, so he was all set.

He opened his front door, only to stumble back at the sight of the man standing there. Russell had his fist up as if he'd been about to knock, and he beamed when he saw Cyril. "There you are. My favorite necromancer."

Russell was careful as he leaned down to hug Cyril, and Cyril hugged him back. He was still getting used to the amount of physical contact he was getting from Vale and Russell, but he liked it. It was just a lot after a life spent only hugging his mother.

"Where are you going?" Russell asked, looking at the bag swung over Cyril's shoulder.

"On a job."

"And Vale's letting you go without him?"

"He called me. He's the one who wants me to reanimate someone."

There was a moment of silence before Russell guffawed. "Really? How did that happen?"

"I don't know. He just said that he found something weird after taking care of his target, and he wants me to reanimate the guy. You should come with me. I'm sure he'll want to talk to you, anyway."

"Oh, I'm not about to miss that. You can bet your ass that I'm coming with you."

Cyril wasn't surprised, and Vale wouldn't be when he saw Russell there, either. He'd roll his eyes and huff and puff, but he trusted Russell with his life. Hell, he'd probably be happy that Cyril hadn't had to come alone.

Cyril let Russell take over since this was what he did for a living. He handed over his phone so Russell could check the address, then climbed into Russell's car. Music blasted as soon as Russell turned on the engine, and Cyril reached over to lower the volume, but Russell didn't seem to mind. He sang along to the music, looking like a regular guy rather than a professional killer who could eliminate Cyril in about a dozen different ways without breaking a sweat.

They didn't speak much as they drove to where Vale was. Russell became much more serious as soon as they got to the hotel, and by the time they were out of the car, it was like being with a completely different person.

"Stay close to me," Russell ordered as they made their way through the lobby.

Luckily, no one tried to stop them. Hell, no one even looked at them. Cyril still obeyed and stuck close to Russell, just in case.

He was relieved when they got into the elevator and even more so once they stepped out of it. Russell quickly found the room number Vale had given them, as if it wasn't the first time he'd been in this hotel. Maybe it wasn't. Russell had lived in hotels for the past few months, ever since he'd decided to move to be closer to Vale. He'd complained it wasn't easy to find an apartment when he was always traveling for work, and it wasn't like he could move in with Vale and Cyril. Cyril's apartment was barely big enough for two, let alone for three.

Russell made Cyril stand to the side of the door when they reached the right number. He knocked. Cyril held his breath, wondering what they'd find on the other side. When the door swung open and Vale stood there, looking unharmed, Cyril relaxed.

"You really had to bring him?" Vale asked Cyril as he waved them in.

"I didn't really have a choice. He was about to knock on our door when I opened it, and I couldn't lie to him."

"You could have," Vale said. "You just didn't want to."

"That's because he loves me," Russell said. "So? What happened?"

"I'm not sure. The job seemed normal. I got here, killed the target, and was ready to leave, but I bumped into the coffee table, and some documents fell to the floor."

Russell clicked his tongue. "That's not like you."

"The target was a slob and left his shoes in the way. Anyway, when I looked at the documents, I saw a picture of one of my old targets. Artemis told me that I'd been hired to kill this guy because he'd killed someone's father, and after seeing this picture, I'm wondering if that's all there is to it."

"Whose picture was that?"

"John West."

The name didn't mean anything to Cyril, but it clearly did to Russell because he grimaced. "I remember you killed that guy. He had a son, right?"

"He did."

"And you think that this guy hired you to kill John West and the son wanted him dead for that?"

Vale shook his head. "That's not what happened. John West's son was the one who hired me to kill his father. This is not John West's son."

They stared at each other for a moment. There was nothing Cyril could do, so he shuffled his feet and waited for Vale to need him. Vale gestured toward the bathroom, and Cyril was glad to be able to get to work. He felt a little weird, standing there discussing targets and hits.

He stepped into the bathroom, wondering what he'd find, but it was clear that Vale had cleaned up while waiting for him. The target had been taking a shower, but Vale had covered his naked body and gotten him out of the stall. The man was stretched out on the carpet now, mostly dry, with a hole in his head.

Cyril was used to reanimating people who'd been killed with bullets, so it didn't faze him. He got to work, easily ignoring the fact that his boyfriend had been the one to kill this guy. If the guy was bad, Cyril didn't have a problem with his death. If he was a good person, it had clearly been a mistake, and Cyril would reanimate him anyway.

"Ready?" he asked without looking behind himself.

"Ready," Russell said, sounding gleeful.

Cyril rolled his eyes, but he had work to do. He focused on

his patient, gently touching the man's wrist and pushing his magic into his body. He found the bullet still lodged in the man's skull and gently pushed it out. He could leave it in, but it might change the man's personality, which was something he tried to avoid as much as he could. It only took a bit of magic for him to get rid of the bullet, anyway.

His ability worked better on people who didn't have foreign objects inside of them, especially when that foreign object had killed them. It was almost as if it wanted to help him get rid of the bullet, and once it appeared at the open wound, he gently picked it up and put it aside. Then he started on the real work.

It didn't take long. Eventually, the man's eyes blinked open, and he looked at Cyril. His eyes widened. Cyril had been through plenty of these, so he expected it when the man started screaming.

They all did in the beginning.

Vale winced when the man started screaming. He reached down and slapped a hand against the man's mouth, but unfortunately, that probably did more damage than anything. The man started freaking out even more, scrambling to get away from Vale, trying to push him away at the same time as he crab-walked the short length of the bathroom.

"You should probably leave this to Cyril," Russell said, sounding amused.

Vale didn't have a choice, so he let go. The man's back hit the wall, and he whimpered. His eyes were wide as he took in the three men standing in the bathroom.

Vale took a step back, happy to let his boyfriend take control. He wasn't sure the guy had recognized him yet, but if he hadn't, he probably would soon. Then he'd scream even louder, which wasn't something they could afford considering they were in a hotel.

Cyril crouched in front of the man and raised his hands in a comforting gesture. "Hi. My name is Cyril, and I'm a necromancer. I just reanimated you."

The man's wide eyes turned to Cyril. He didn't shy away from him when Cyril gently touched his shoulder, which was good because if he had, Vale would have killed him a second time.

"I know this is a shock, especially because your death was unexpected. Can you tell me more about you? Do you remember who you are?" Cyril asked.

"Robbie," the man croaked. He cleared his throat. "My name is Robbie. What happened? Why am I naked, and why are you here?"

Cyril grabbed the nearest towel and wrapped it around Robbie's shoulders. Vale wanted to start asking more pointed questions, but Russell was right. He should give Cyril the space to do his job. He knew what he was doing, and he was good at it. If Vale wanted answers, he'd have to wait until Robbie wasn't screaming his head off anymore.

"You were in the shower when you were killed," Cyril gently explained. "I got the bullet out, so it won't cause you trouble."

Robbie raised a trembling hand to his forehead, but Cyril caught it before he could touch the wound. "You don't need to do that right now. I want to make sure you're all right."

"How can I be all right? I have no idea what happened. Why did I die? Who shot me?"

Vale raised his hand. "That would be me. I was paid to kill you."

That was definitely the wrong thing to say. Robbie paled so badly that if he hadn't been sitting down, Vale would've been afraid he'd fall on his face. Robbie tried to back away from Vale, but he was stuck against the wall.

Cyril glared at Vale. "He's not going to hurt you," he tried to soothe.

"He killed me," Robbie croaked.

"Not because he's a bad person. Someone paid him to kill you."

"Who does that?"

"Professional killers," Russell said with a smile. He leaned down toward Robbie. "Hi. My name is Russell, and I didn't kill you. I also didn't reanimate you."

Robbie blinked. "Why are you here, then?"

"That's something I wonder every day," Vale muttered.

This was starting to take too long. There was no way to know if anyone in the hotel was aware of what had happened, and Vale didn't want to stay here any longer than they absolutely had to. He crouched next to Robbie, trying to ignore how frightened the man was of him. He understood why. Not only was he a professional killer, but he'd also killed Robbie fifteen or so minutes ago. Anyone else in Robbie's place would be ready to run away screaming, and Vale wouldn't blame them. He wouldn't blame Robbie for doing so, but he needed answers.

"I was paid to kill you," he explained. "It's nothing personal, and you don't have to worry that I'll do it again. I was leaving the room when I knocked against the coffee table. Why do you have a picture of John West? When I accepted the hit on your head, I was told that you killed a man's father and that he was hiring me to get revenge."

Robbie gaped. "I didn't kill anyone."

"I believe you. I'm just trying to understand what happened. I don't kill innocent people, and if someone manipulated me to hurt you when you had nothing to blame yourself for, I'm going to be pissed."

Robbie cowered, but Cyril was there, soothing him again. Vale wasn't angry at Robbie—the poor man hadn't done anything—but he was annoyed and restless. He didn't like the situation he'd stepped into, and he could tell this wouldn't be the last he'd see of Robbie and whoever had hired Vale to kill him.

"Do you have any idea who could have hired Roux to kill you?" Russell asked.

Robbie swallowed heavily. "I know who did it."

"Tell me, and I'll make sure they can't hurt you ever again," Vale said with a growl. Whoever it was wouldn't be able to hurt Robbie again because they'd be fucking dead.

"You said you know John West," Robbie started. "Well, I'm sure you know he died a few years ago. I wasn't the one who killed him. His son did, and I found out. I have proof."

Shit. If Robbie had proof that Peter West had his father killed, he'd probably threatened to go to the authorities. It explained why someone—probably Peter West—had put out a hit on him.

"So Peter West hired Vale to kill you," Russell offered.

"I don't know, but I wouldn't be surprised. He knows I know, and the last time I saw him, he said he was going to clean up loose ends. I'm pretty sure it was a threat."

Vale had no doubt it was, because no matter how you looked at this mess, Robbie was definitely a loose end.

CHAPTER THREE

V ale's phone was in his hand before he even left the bathroom. There was only one person he needed to talk to right now who wasn't already here.

"What's wrong?" Artemis asked when she answered. "You already emailed me with the details."

"I didn't have all of them when I did. What do you know about the target?"

"Not much, but I do know that I'm not going to like whatever's happening."

Vale could hear the clicking of her keyboard. He didn't have to be there to know what she was doing.

"I have a name and a short biography," Artemis explained. "The person who put the hit up mentioned that the target killed his father or had him killed and that he wanted the target to pay for that."

Vale sat in the chair under the window. "I'm pretty sure that the client is Peter West."

It took a moment before Artemis reacted. "*The* Peter West?"

"Yes, the one who hired me to kill his father."

"If he's the person who hired you to do that, why is he saying that this Robbie guy did it?"

"Because apparently, Robbie knows that Peter had his father killed and was ready to go to the authorities. Now, Peter's planning on cleaning up loose ends."

"Well, you just did that for him."

Vale grimaced. "Not really. I had Cyril reanimate Robbie."

22

There was a moment of silence. Vale was pretty sure that Artemis thought he was an idiot, and she wouldn't be wrong. What had he been thinking, reanimating his target? He'd needed answers, but surely there would have been another way to find them.

Or maybe not. Technically, Vale could be seen as a loose end. He'd been the one who killed John West, and he knew who had hired him to do so. Peter West had insisted on meeting with him before Vale did the job, so he knew who Vale was, and it looked like he'd managed to find him, although it didn't look like he'd done so on purpose. Vale was sure that other assassins had applied for the job, since it was well-paid. The fact that he'd been chosen might mean that Peter West was trying to get to him, but it also might simply mean that Artemis had been quicker than other handlers.

"That doesn't sound like a smart decision," Artemis said. "Especially since I confirmed that the target was dead after I got your email."

"I don't really care what you confirmed or didn't confirm. I had to know what was going on, and it's a shit show."

"I'm sorry I didn't look further into this. Robbie is innocent?"

"He didn't do anything. I don't know what he has to do with all of this beyond finding out that West had his father killed, but he looks like he wouldn't hurt a fly."

"Looks don't always mean much."

"In this case, I think it does. I was hired to kill an innocent man. I don't like that I was manipulated into it and that Peter West knows me. I need to know more about this. I want to know why he decided to set up this entire thing."

"I'll look into it, but it doesn't sound like there's much more to find out. Peter West hired you to kill his father a few years ago. Now, he hired you and lied to you when he told you that you were supposed to kill the man who'd killed John

West."

"That's what I don't get. Why hire me, of all people? I'm one of the few who knows what actually happened when John West died, so why pull me back in?"

"I'll look into it."

"Please do. In the meantime, I'm going to take Cyril home."

They hung up, and Vale looked up to find Russell hovering close by. He was smiling because he was an idiot who smiled even in dire situations, but seeing him helped soothe something in Vale.

Whatever was going on, Vale wouldn't be dealing with it alone. Russell might act like an idiot most of the time, but he was smart and professional when he was working. More importantly, he liked Cyril and would protect him with his life.

Because whoever was behind all of this wouldn't hesitate to use Cyril as leverage against Vale. If they had Cyril, Vale would do pretty much anything they asked.

"She'll look into it?" Russell asked.

"Yeah. She's not sure what's happening either."

"Well, Robbie said that Peter West is cleaning up, and since you're the one who killed his father, it makes sense that he'd want to clean *you* up, too."

"So what? He's going to hire a professional assassin to kill a professional assassin?"

Russell shrugged. "Weirder things have happened. Watch your back, all right?"

Vale got up and clasped Russell's shoulder. "I don't have to watch my back, because you're already watching it."

Russell winked. "Until Peter West hires me to kill you."

They walked back into the bathroom, where Cyril was still fussing over Robbie. Vale wanted nothing more than to take him home. If Peter West was after him, he might find out about Cyril, and that wasn't something Vale could allow to happen. He needed to protect Cyril, and he couldn't do that in a hotel room bathroom.

"Let's go home," he offered as he reached for Cyril.

"You're abandoning me?" Robbie asked, scrambling to get to his feet.

"You should go home."

"So I can be killed again?" Robbie chuckled darkly. "You think you'll be the only guy Peter West hired to kill me?"

He was right. If Peter really wanted Robbie dead, he'd put out more hits on him. For now, he thought that Vale had killed Robbie, but that wouldn't last forever, even if they kept Robbie hidden.

But Robbie wasn't Vale's responsibility. Vale had made a mistake by killing him, but Cyril had fixed it, and Vale didn't owe Robbie anything else.

"I guess you'd better start hiding," he said as he tugged Cyril closer.

Cyril was frowning. One look at his face was enough for Vale to know what he was about to say next. He shook his head, stepping away.

"No. We don't have the space."

"But he's in hiding. He can't go home or to his family. These killers would too easily find him there, and we can't let him die."

"Again," Robbie grumbled.

Vale glared at him. Luckily, that was enough for Robbie to snap his mouth shut. Vale was reaching the end of his patience, and while none of this was Robbie's fault, he was the easiest target for Vale's anger. "Look, I just did my job," he said.

"Which is to kill people."

"It is, so I'd watch my mouth if I were you."

Robbie and Vale glared at each other. Vale could see that Robbie was still afraid, but he was impressed because the man was standing up to him. He'd already killed Robbie once, yet

Robbie was still snapping back at him.

"He'll come home with us," Cyril declared.

Vale groaned. He should've known this would happen. He *had* known this would happen. "Where are you going to put him?"

"The couch will be fine for a few nights until we find something more permanent and look into the situation." Cyril grabbed Robbie's hand and squeezed. "Don't worry. You'll be safe with us."

Russell started laughing, and when Vale glared at him, he quickly turned it into a cough. He was laughing so hard that it made him sound like he was dying, and for a moment, Vale found himself hoping he would. He'd miss his best friend, though.

"Fine, but if I hear one word of complaint out of his mouth, he's out," he said with a growl.

Cyril beamed at Vale as if he'd just offered him the moon. When he did that, Vale's knees went a little weak, and he had to resist the urge to kiss him silly. He wanted to, but it was too dangerous. He and Russell needed to get Robbie and Cyril out of this room and the hotel entirely before Peter West realized something was wrong.

Still, when Cyril leaned closer to kiss Vale's cheek, Vale pulled him closer for a moment. He nuzzled his cheek on top of Cyril's head, inhaling Cyril's strawberry and mint shampoo and telling himself that no matter what happened, he'd always have this.

"Wait, the two of you are together?" Robbie asked.

Vale groaned. This was going to be a long time, whatever the length of time Robbie would be staying with them.

Cyril was glad they were taking Robbie home with them. It was clear that the poor man was terrified, and Cyril was afraid that if they left him there, he'd end up dying again. It wouldn't be Vale this time, though, which meant that Robbie would actually die.

Cyril felt sorry for him. They still weren't sure what was happening, but it was clear that Robbie had been trying to do the right thing and had been killed instead. Cyril didn't blame Vale since he hadn't been given all the information, but he knew Vale blamed himself. Cyril was glad that his boyfriend was considering retirement. He just wished Vale didn't have to deal with such a messy situation before making his decision.

"We need to get you packed up," Vale told Robbie. "The sooner we're out of here, the better. For now, West thinks that you're dead, but that's not going to last long. You don't want to be here when he finds out you're very much alive."

Robbie tried getting up, but it was clear that he was still shaky, so Cyril rushed over to help him. He ignored Vale's little scowl, knowing it had more to do with the situation than with what he was doing for Robbie. Vale was pissed because someone had manipulated him into killing an innocent man, and if Cyril knew anything about him, it was that he was very selective when it came to choosing his jobs.

Even though he was a professional killer, Vale wasn't a bad person. He didn't want to kill people who didn't deserve it. Cyril would rather he not kill anyone, but he understood how evil the world could be. He knew that some people didn't deserve to be alive, and he was glad to know there was someone out there taking care of them.

Of course, it was a job for Vale, not a life mission or anything like that, but that didn't change the fact that by killing bad people, he and Russell made the world a little bit safer. As soon as Vale had realized that something was wrong, he'd had Cyril reanimate Robbie. If he hadn't done that, Robbie would be dead, and his family would be grieving.

They still might. Robbie couldn't go back to them, no matter how much he wanted to. Keeping him at the apartment wasn't going to be easy, but they didn't have a choice.

They went back into the bedroom. Robbie was still wrapped in the towel and walked as if his legs were unsteady. Russell and Vale were quietly talking in a corner but stopped as soon as Robbie walked in. Robbie looked from Vale to Russell, then, to everyone's surprise, let go of Cyril and hooked an arm around Russell's. "I think I need help."

Russell slowly nodded. "Of course. What do you need me to do?"

Cyril smiled and turned away. Russell had everything under control. If they wanted to get out of here as soon as possible, he should start packing Robbie's stuff.

He stayed away from anything Robbie might need to dress and started packing away the rest. It was awkward because it wasn't his stuff, but he suspected that Robbie would be happy to have all of it with him once they reached the apartment.

Cyril could see that Vale was impatient, and he didn't blame him. He knew enough to be aware of the fact that the longer they spent there, the higher the possibility someone would discover them. He still couldn't find it in himself to rush Robbie.

But eventually they left the hotel room. Robbie was behind Cyril and Vale, clinging to Russell's arm as if he was afraid Russell would disappear and leave him alone with Vale and Cyril. For some reason, Vale must have found it hilarious, but he waited to say something about it until they were out of the hotel. "I guess you're fine going with Russell?" he asked Robbie.

Robbie nodded. "He's the only normal one here. No offense, Cyril, because you're nice, but you're a necromancer, and that's a little weird. There's also the whole *I was dead half an hour ago* thing that I can't quite wrap my mind around."

"It's fine," Cyril assured him.

Vale knew how much Cyril hated it when people judged him because he was a necromancer, and that was what Robbie was doing, but Cyril wasn't offended. Clearly Vale was, because he decided to get a little revenge.

"You know, it's funny that you say that Russell is the only normal one between all of us because we do the same job."

Robbie's eyes widened, and he took a step away from Russell, who glared at Vale. "You really had to say that?"

Vale grinned at him. "I really did. Have fun on the way home."

"I changed my mind," Robbie said. "Cyril, I want to come with you."

"Pity, because he's coming with me," Vale said as he wrapped an arm around Cyril's shoulders and led him in the direction of his car.

"That was mean," Cyril told him once they were alone.

"What was mean was what he said to you. You're not weird. You're the sweetest man I've ever known."

Cyril leaned harder against Vale's side. "That's really nice."

"You know me. I'm a nice guy all around."

"I know. That's why you agreed to have Robbie stay with us for a little bit."

They might regret it depending on what would happen next, but Cyril didn't regret it, and he knew Vale would do pretty much anything for him, including protecting a stranger just because Cyril asked him to.

Cyril was the luckiest man in the world. Vale had given him his love and his trust, and he hoped he would never lose them. He didn't know what he'd do if he lost Vale, which meant they needed to fix the mess Peter West had created.

CHAPTER FOUR

Artemis called back after they got home. Cyril wanted to know what was happening, but it was more important to him to help Robbie settle in. Vale would tell him what Artemis had found, anyway.

"So this is it," Cyril said as he waved at the apartment. "It's not big, and you'll have to take the couch, but no one should be able to find you here. They won't expect you to be staying with the guy who killed you."

"I can't believe I'm doing this," Robbie muttered.

He stood in the middle of the living room, his arms wrapped around himself, his eyes a little wide. Cyril had never died, but he'd seen death and reanimations enough times that he suspected he knew a bit about how Robbie felt.

Robbie's life had ended, only to be given back to him. He still had someone coming after him, and they'd probably try to kill him again once they found out he wasn't dead. If Cyril was in his place, he'd be screaming and crying, but Robbie had calmed down, and now, he just looked tired.

"Russell and Vale will protect you. I'll do what I can, too, but I'm not like them. I'm just a necromancer."

"You saved me."

Cyril shrugged. "Not really."

"You literally brought me back to life. If it wasn't for you, I wouldn't be here right now—hell, I wouldn't be anywhere. I would be *dead*."

"I know it's a lot to process, but you'll have time to do that here, all right? You can stay for as long as you need."

"I don't think your boyfriend's gonna be happy with that."

"Even if he's not happy, he'll indulge me."

Robbie stared. "You don't care that he kills people for a living?"

"I know death. I've seen it time and time again, and it doesn't disturb me. Besides, Vale and his handler do everything they can to ensure that the only people he kills are people who deserve it. You were a glitch in that system, and Vale hates himself for what he did to you. If he'd known, he wouldn't have hurt you, but he's trying to fix it."

"Because he wants answers."

"He didn't know anything about you when he killed you. Even if he'd had all the information he's looking for now, he would have asked me to help you. I know it's weird, but he's not a bad person."

Robbie sighed. "Right now, I don't have any idea what's happening, and I don't trust my judgment. I guess I'll have to trust yours."

"I don't know about that since he's my boyfriend, but I like to think I wouldn't be with him if he were a bad person." Even though Vale was the only person who'd ever shown so much interest in Cyril.

That wasn't why Cyril was with him. He was with Vale because Vale was a good person, and Cyril wanted to get to know him and spend the rest of his life with him.

But they were in trouble once again. What was it with them and people coming after them? For now, no one wanted to kill Vale, but Cyril suspected that wouldn't last long. If what Robbie had said was right and Peter West was trying to clean up loose ends, he might view Vale as one of them.

The skittering sound of Oscar rushing closer made Cyril smile. He crouched just in time for Oscar to turn the corner and launch himself into his arms. Cyril caught him easily and kissed the top of Oscar's head, then turned to Robbie.

Who looked horrified and was gaping at him. "What the fuck is that?"

"My pet, Oscar."

"That's not a pet. That's a skull."

"I reanimated him." Cyril held Oscar close. "Don't offend him, please. This is his home as much as it's mine and Vale's."

Robbie swallowed. "What the fuck happened to my life?" he asked. "It was normal, and then I decided that I needed to stick my nose into something that was none of my business, and here I am."

Cyril was pretty sure he wasn't talking to him anymore.

"I'll be nice to your pet," Robbie said, but the way he was looking at Oscar told Cyril that maybe he needed to keep the two separated.

It wasn't going to be easy, because Oscar was curious and used to having free rein in the apartment. Even Vale was used to him, so Cyril didn't keep an eye on him anymore.

It looked like that was about to change.

"I'm going to go," Russell said as he came closer to stroke Oscar's head. "Artemis has everything under control, so I wouldn't worry too much. No one knows that Robbie's here, which means he should be safe and that you can all sleep well tonight. If you need anything, though, Cyril, you know I'm only a phone call away."

Cyril nodded and hugged Russell with one arm. "Thanks for being there for us."

"Always. You're my family." Russell turned his attention to Robbie. "Which means that if you hurt Cyril, I'll hurt you."

"I'm not planning on doing anything to him," Robbie assured him.

"I meant emotionally, too. Cyril might be a necromancer, but he's a nice person, and he doesn't deserve people treating him badly just because of what he can do."

Robbie raised his hands. "He literally brought me back to

life. I'm not going to be nasty to him or anything like that. I'm just overwhelmed and a little all over the place emotionally."

Which Cyril could understand. He patted Robbie's shoulder, relieved when Robbie didn't step away.

It would take some time to get used to living with Robbie, but Cyril wanted to keep him safe. What had happened to him wasn't right, and until Vale fixed it, Robbie would be staying with them.

Just in case.

Vale was exhausted by the time he and Cyril finally managed to go to bed. It felt odd to have someone else in the apartment. It had taken Vale some time to get used to living with Cyril, but they'd found a nice balance, and now, all of that had gone to shit because Robbie was here.

Vale sighed as he slumped on the edge of the bed. He didn't regret having Robbie with them. He felt a bit guilty about killing him, even though he then had him reanimated. He shouldn't have killed him in the first place. He wouldn't have if he'd known what was happening, but he hadn't. He did now, and he wanted to make things right. He supposed that one way to do that was to give Robbie a safe place where he could lay low until all of this blew over.

Cyril stepped into the bedroom and closed the door. He was wearing a pair of soft pajama pants with unicorns on them and a t-shirt that Vale was pretty sure belonged to him because it was too big to be Cyril's. Like always, seeing Cyril in his clothes gave Vale a thrill. He already knew Cyril was his, but like this, it was even more obvious.

Vale still wasn't sure what he'd done to deserve a man like Cyril, but he would cherish him for the rest of his life. It was the least Cyril deserved.

"You think Robbie will be okay tonight?" Cyril asked as he

slid under the blankets.

He looked worried, which wasn't a surprise. He always worried about people, which was one of the things Vale liked so much about him.

"He'll be fine. I'll put cameras outside the apartment tomorrow, but for tonight, Russell agreed to keep an eye on the building from his car, and there's Oscar. He'd freak out anyone who tries coming in, and if we hear screaming, we'll know to run."

Cyril settled against his pillow and turned to his side so he could watch Vale. "You think someone will find him?"

"I doubt it. No one knows he's here. Why would the assassin who killed him bring him home?"

That earned him a little smile. "I guess. Thank you for doing that for him. You didn't have to, and I know you don't like having strangers in your personal space."

"I don't, but I feel guilty about what I did to him." Vale got to his feet and pulled off his t-shirt. He decided to keep his sweatpants on, just in case he had to run out of the bedroom. "I did kill him, after all."

"You wouldn't have if you'd known what was happening. That's not you."

Vale slipped into the bed next to his boyfriend and pulled him close. He kissed Cyril's forehead, inhaled his scent, and felt something inside of him settle. "You're too good for me."

"I don't think so. I think I'm just the right amount of good for you."

Vale grinned. "Are you?"

"You deserve to be loved, Vale. I know that sometimes, you feel like you don't because of your job and everything else, but you're not a bad person."

"Plenty of people would think I am considering my job."

Cyril was silent for a moment.

Vale gave him time to think. He was slightly afraid of what

his boyfriend would say, but he shouldn't have been.

"I know death," Cyril eventually said. "Mostly, my job is pretty normal. I get called because people lost a loved one and need to talk to them one last time, or maybe they want me to reanimate them completely. Sometimes, though, things are worse."

"Like they were when you were kidnapped."

Cyril shuddered in Vale's arms. "Exactly. Some people want to reanimate others for bad reasons, and while I try to stay away from those jobs, sometimes, I can't. I'm lucky that nothing bad ever happened to me, but I know there are bad people in the world. I know that while I wish that all of them were redeemable, that's not the case, and they would be dangerous if they were left alone. I also know that the authorities can't always punish the people who deserve it, and the only alternative is to leave them at large to hurt other people."

Vale ran his hand up and down Cyril's back. "I feel like you're romanticizing my job. I don't just kill monsters, Cyril."

"Maybe not, but you don't kill anyone who doesn't deserve it."

That much was true, but Vale was still certain that some people wouldn't see it like that. Then, there were the mistakes, like what had happened with Robbie. He hadn't deserved to die, and if Vale hadn't known Cyril, Robbie would be gone.

Robbie didn't deserve that. Vale was glad to have Cyril in his life. He was loved, but more importantly, having Cyril meant that Robbie was alive. It was still another dark mark on Vale's soul. He doubted it would make a difference, but then, he didn't believe in heaven and hell. He didn't believe in anything after death, but he still always tried to do the right thing.

Cyril pressed closer and hooked his arms around Vale's neck. The way he looked at him made Vale feel loved, which wasn't something that often happened to him. He still didn't feel like he deserved any of this, but he was selfish and greedy. If Cyril wanted to give him this, Vale would take it.

"I love you," Cyril murmured. "I know all of you. I know what you did in the past, and I still love you."

"And I love you."

The pleased little smile that appeared on Cyril's face told Vale that it had been the right thing to say. He couldn't pull Cyril any closer, but he could kiss him, so he did.

He never wanted this to end. He knew he'd have to retire when this mess was over, if anything so he could keep Cyril safe. He wouldn't have done it for anyone else, but he truly did love Cyril, and Cyril deserved to be safe and happy. That wouldn't happen until Vale quit his job, and he was ready to do so more than ever.

First, though, he'd have to get rid of Peter West. Once that was done, Vale could leave everything behind and focus on his future.

The future he was holding in his arms, the future who moaned when Vale pushed a hand under his t-shirt.

The future who would have to stay quiet if they didn't want Robbie to hear what they were about to do.

CHAPTER FIVE

Vale stepped out of the grocery store, his arms heavy with bags. He'd remembered to grab Cyril's favorite shower gel and more creamer, so he was pretty pleased with himself. Usually, Cyril enjoyed coming with him to the store, but with everything happening, Vale felt better knowing that his boyfriend was at home. It was safer than being here, but he knew he wouldn't be able to hide Cyril forever. Eventually, Cyril would have to accept a job, which meant leaving the apartment. Vale would go with him, but he was only one man, and there was no way to know how many killers Peter West had hired.

They hadn't heard from him again. Robbie had been living with Vale and Cyril for a few days, which explained why they'd needed groceries. He was a skittish little thing, staying as far away from Vale as possible. Vale didn't blame him considering he'd shot him in the head. He hadn't known Robbie then, and he still didn't know him well, but he knew enough to be sure that Robbie wouldn't hurt a fly, let alone have a guy killed.

The idiot had been trying to do the right thing. From what Vale had gathered, Robbie had been working with John West before Vale killed him. He'd been his assistant, and apparently, he'd really liked his boss, even though Vale was pretty sure that John had never done one legal thing in his life. When he died, Robbie had stayed at the company to help put documents and files in order, which apparently was how he'd found out that John's son, Peter, had been behind the hit on his father.

Vale had been the weapon, but Peter had been the brain.

That was when Robbie had done something stupid. Instead of going straight to the authorities or keeping it to himself, he'd confronted Peter West. He probably didn't know what Peter and John were up to and that they knew worse criminals than Robbie could ever dream of. Maybe he thought that Peter would break down and admit everything. Maybe he believed that Peter would hand himself over to the authorities and pay for what he'd done.

That wasn't what Peter had done. He'd hired a professional killer—Vale—and had Robbie killed. Now, Robbie slept on Vale's couch, ate Vale's food, and looked terrified every time Vale glanced his way. Vale wasn't quite sure what to do about that, but he hoped it wouldn't last much longer.

He opened his trunk and started piling the bags inside. He felt movement behind his back and started to turn, his hand going for his gun.

It was too late. Something hard pressed against his spine, and he froze. Whoever was holding him at gunpoint was smart. They'd waited until he was by his car, which he always parked far away from the doors. There was no one around. The only person Vale could see was a woman in the distance, but she was walking with a child, and there was no way Vale would pull her into this.

"I can see why there's a rumor going around that you're retiring," a woman said.

Vale recognized the voice. He'd only met Calypso in person a few times, but they'd worked together more often than that. Usually, they communicated on the phone.

She was good. She was so good that Vale knew that if she was here to kill him, he was as good as dead. He briefly wondered if Cyril would try reanimating him. It was probably something they needed to talk about, just in case.

"You're getting old," Calypso added.

Vale snorted. "I'm getting distracted by my boyfriend."

"That's why I don't do relationships. Having a boyfriend is going to get you killed."

"Is that why you're here? To kill me?"

The pressure on Vale's back vanished. He quickly turned, but he didn't take his gun out. He reached for it, but he knew Calypso would kill him before he could even touch it, so what use would it be?

Her gun was nowhere to be seen. She stood in front of him, tall and blonde, a smug expression on her face. Her red lips were twisted into a smile, and Vale couldn't shake the feeling that she was laughing at him.

"Did you know there was a hit on your head?" Calypso asked.

Vale did know that. He hadn't been surprised when Artemis had called him to tell him about it. After all, he'd had one of his targets reanimated. That wasn't how a professional killer behaved, especially not when Peter West was involved. "How much?"

Calypso's smile widened. "Way too much for someone like you, if you want to know what I think."

"Not particularly. Are you going to do it?"

Calypso stared at him for a moment. Vale had no idea what it meant. The only friends he'd made in the business were Artemis and Brutus—Rachel and Russell. He might have worked with Calypso, but that didn't make them friends or even friendly.

He didn't blame her for taking the hit on him. He should've been more careful since he knew about it, but he hadn't thought that many professional killers would want to take the bait. They were a community, albeit a strange one, and most of them wouldn't want to kill one of their own.

Most, but not all.

"I will," Calypso confirmed. "But not here, and not now. I'm going to give you a chance to run."

"Why?"

"Because it's more fun. Besides, you should say goodbye to your little boyfriend, because this is the only time I'm warning you. The next time I see you, I'll kill you."

Vale smirked at her. "Or maybe I'll kill you."

"I suppose we'll find out," she said with a wink. "And remember. It's nothing personal."

"It sure feels personal."

"It never is."

That much was true. When it turned personal, it meant that Vale had lost objectivity, which was the most important thing in his job. He couldn't afford emotions to take over. He had to keep a cool head, which had proven itself to be impossible when Cyril was involved.

The sound of a car screeching to a halt made both of them jump. Vale looked away from Calypso for just a second, and when he turned back, she was gone. It was as if she'd never been there. She hadn't left any trace, but Vale didn't need any.

Calypso was after him, and he doubted she'd be the only one. Most of the good professional assassins would probably stay away, but not all of them were good, and some had no morals.

Vale swore. He was going to be hunted by a bunch of idiots, which put Cyril in danger. Vale couldn't allow that, which meant he'd have to start hitting back instead of waiting for them to come to him.

He was going to need help.

Robbie was like a terrified animal. It was more evident when Vale was home, but even when he was only with Cyril, he skulked around corners and tried to hide. It wasn't obvious—

he didn't hide in closets or anything like that—but he tended to go very still and quiet whenever anyone else was in the room, which was awkward since the three of them were stuck in a small apartment.

Cyril wasn't new to people being afraid of him. Usually, it was because of his necromancer ability, but he wasn't sure that was it this time, at least not entirely. Yes, Robbie was probably uncomfortable with the fact that Cyril had brought him back to life, but he seemed absolutely terrified of Vale and, by association, of Cyril. After all, Cyril was Vale's boyfriend. He knew what Vale did for a living and didn't have a problem with it.

Well, not always. He did have a problem with the fact that Vale had killed Robbie, but that hadn't been Vale's fault.

He wasn't sure Robbie believed that.

He peeked into the living room. At least Robbie wasn't afraid of Oscar anymore. He'd taken to him almost instantly once he'd agreed to touch him, and he spent most of his time on the couch cuddling him. Oscar was over the moon happy to have someone handle him like that, and it meant he spent less time hounding Vale around the apartment, which made Vale happy. He still wasn't used to Oscar, even though he'd been living here longer than Robbie.

The front door banged open, making Cyril and Robbie jump. For a moment, Cyril's heart raced, and he was convinced that someone was here to kill him. Then, he realized that if a killer was here for someone, it would be Robbie, so he quickly rushed into the living room.

Vale came in, carrying several bags. He didn't pause and didn't say anything to Robbie. He went straight toward the kitchen, so Cyril stepped aside to let him in.

"Did something happen at the grocery store?" he asked because it was the only explanation he could think of.

"Yeah, something fucking happened," Vale said with a

growl. "Can you put away the groceries?"

"Of course. Whatever you need."

Vale's expression softened. "I don't know what I'd do without you." He hooked an arm around Cyril's shoulders and pulled him close to kiss his forehead.

"Luckily for you, you'll never have to find out."

"I hope not." Vale sucked in a breath and gently pulled away. "I have to call Artemis."

Since he was calling Rachel with her codename, it meant it involved work. He'd said something had happened at the grocery store, and between those two things, Cyril was suddenly even more nervous.

Thankfully, it looked like Vale was planning to make his call in the kitchen, because he leaned against the kitchen island while taking his phone out. Cyril went to work, but he kept one ear open because he wanted to know what had spooked Vale so badly.

"Hey," Vale said, lowering his phone and putting it on speaker.

Cyril was grateful for that, especially when he hadn't asked him to.

"Calypso accosted me in the grocery store parking lot."

Cyril had no idea who Calypso was, but from the way Rachel sucked in a breath, he could guess she wasn't their friend.

"You're still alive," Rachel said.

"Very funny." Vale paused. "I'm alive because she didn't try to kill me. She was there to warn me that there's a hit on me and that she's taking it."

"We already knew that."

They did. Cyril had been freaking out since Rachel had called to tell them about it. He'd known something like this would happen. At the thought that Vale might have never returned from the grocery store, he felt himself going faint.

He'd known what he was getting into when he'd started

dating Vale. He'd known that Vale's job was dangerous and that there was a chance that someday, he wouldn't return. It had been easy to ignore, especially since Cyril was planning on reanimating Vale if he ever died, but he couldn't anymore. It was all in front of him now, and he had to listen to Vale explain what had happened in the grocery store parking lot and what Calypso had said.

What would he do if something happened to Vale? He'd survived on his own before, so he knew he could do so again, but he didn't want to. He didn't want to go back to living without friends. He loved his mother, but he was an adult, and he couldn't cling to her the way he had before. Besides, he doubted he'd lose Rachel and Russell, even if something did happen to Vale. He was stuck with them, which was a lovely thought.

"Yeah," Vale said. "She just disappeared, but I don't expect her to be so nice the next time we cross paths. You need to make me a list of people who will be coming after me."

Cyril was frightened. It was clear that whoever Calypso was, she was only the first in a long line of professional assassins who would be coming for Vale. What if one of them succeeded? What if one of them managed to kill Vale?

"I'll go over the forum and email you," Rachel said.

"Yes, thank you," Vale said. "I'll be waiting with bated breath."

He hung up, closed his eyes, and tilted his face toward the ceiling. "I really didn't need this."

"I don't think anyone ever needs a hit on their head. Are you all right?"

Vale looked at Cyril, grabbed his wrist, and pulled him closer. He wrapped his arms around him, and Cyril felt him inhale deeply.

"I'm all right now that I'm with you," Vale said.

When he said things like that so easily, it made Cyril want

to scream and bury himself inside of him at the same time. Vale was romantic without even trying, while Cyril was awkward on the best of days.

"Is there anything I can do?" Cyril asked.

Vale shook his head. "We can only wait and see. It'll probably be better if I stay at the apartment for the next few days. Russell can grab us whatever we need from the grocery store."

"I'll refuse any job that comes my way," Cyril said.

"I don't want you to feel like you have to do that. People come to you because they need help."

"And normally, I would help them in any way I could, but these aren't normal circumstances. You're my boyfriend, and I'm not leaving you when you're in danger." Cyril could think of nothing worse than going on a job and coming home to Vale hurt, or worse, dead. He didn't want to risk it.

"We'll make a decision if someone calls, all right?" Vale suggested.

Cyril nodded because that was fine with him. He already knew that if anyone contacted him, he would tell them that right now he couldn't come. His job was important, and he felt sorry about refusing any of them, but Vale was more important. Cyril needed to be with him.

And he would be.

Chapter Six

Vale was pissed and needed to do something. He couldn't keep on hiding in the apartment, both because it wasn't like him and because he, Cyril, and Robbie were going to kill each other. The place was too small for three grown men, especially when one of them was terrified of the other two.

Vale couldn't just stay and wait for Peter West to take down the hit he'd put on his head. That would never happen. The only way out of it was to die or to kill West, which wasn't a bad idea.

"That's your murder face," Russell said.

Because as if the apartment wasn't tiny enough, Russell had started spending a lot of time there, too. That meant that *four* grown men were sharing a tiny space, and Vale was ready to start screaming.

"That's because I'm thinking of murdering you," Vale snapped at his best friend.

Russell cocked his head and continued staring. "No, that's not it."

Vale blinked. "What do you mean?"

"You also have an *I'm going to murder Russell* face, and that's not it."

"I have a *I'm going to murder you* face?"

Russell waved at Vale's face again. "Yeah, like that."

Vale got to his feet. He and Russell had been trying to watch a movie while Cyril and Robbie were in the kitchen, but he didn't even know what movie Russell had chosen. He couldn't focus on anything, let alone sit on the couch for two and a half hours.

"I need to do something," he said as he started pacing in front of Russell. Unfortunately, there wasn't a lot of space for him to pace, and he had to turn back after just a few steps.

"You're doing it."

"I didn't mean pacing or hiding or whatever you were thinking. I can't just sit here and wait for one of these assholes to come and kill me. I need to go to the source. That way, I can nip it in the bud and make sure that West won't ruin my life."

Normally, Russell would be on board with whatever idiotic idea Vale came up with, but he seemed subdued this time. "Cyril isn't going to like this," he said.

Vale grimaced. "I know. I wouldn't do it if I didn't think it was the best way for me to make it out alive. If we can get West to drop the hit, I won't have to worry anymore."

"And you think you can do that? Because he's a dick, and a powerful one at that."

"I know, and I'm pretty sure he's not going to drop the hit just because I ask him nicely, but I have to try. Maybe threatening him will help."

"Doesn't sound like a good idea, which means I'm in."

Vale grinned. "I knew you were an idiot."

"I'm not even offended. When are we going?"

"There's no time like the present, right?"

"If Cyril weren't so nice, he'd kill you."

"He'll be worried, but he'll understand. He wants me to be safe as much as I want him to be."

"You're gonna have to tell him, though."

Vale glanced toward the kitchen. "I will." He'd never leave the apartment without telling Cyril. He didn't want his boyfriend to freak out because he couldn't find him, especially considering the circumstances.

He got to his feet and called out for Cyril to join him in their bedroom. He could tell Cyril knew something was about to happen from his expression, and when he opened his arms, Cyril dove into them.

"You're going out," Cyril said, clinging to Vale.

"I have to. With Calypso in the mix, I can't afford to hide and hope that she and the others won't find me. I can't put you or myself in danger like that."

"Do I want to know what you're planning?"

"Probably not. Russell will be with me, though."

"I'm not sure that's a good thing."

Vale snickered. "Maybe not, but at least I won't be alone. I know that telling you not to worry is useless, but try not to, all right? I'm not planning to do anything stupid, and I have every intention of coming back to you."

"I won't try to stop you, because I know this is something you need to do, but I'll be thinking about you."

Vale kissed the top of Cyril's head. "I'm always thinking about you."

Cyril pushed away. "Then go and come back to me quickly. I'm cooking dinner."

Vale didn't know what he'd done to deserve a man like Cyril, but he'd do anything in his power to keep him safe and happy. That meant coming back.

He had every intention of doing just that.

After kissing Cyril one last time, Vale grabbed Russell, and they headed out. Russell drove, which was a relief because Vale wasn't sure he could focus on the road. He trusted his best friend to get him where he needed to go. Hell, he trusted Russell to watch his back and ensure he made it out alive.

And if he didn't, he trusted Russell to take care of Cyril.

As soon as Vale left the apartment, Cyril went to work because he had to keep busy. If he didn't, he'd start freaking out about what was happening to Vale, and he couldn't stand doing that for hours. He had no idea how long Vale would be gone, but until he was home, it was better for him to stay distracted.

That was where Robbie found him about half an hour later. He'd quickly stepped back into the living room after Vale and Russell had left, abandoning Cyril in the kitchen. That was fine with Cyril, although he would have enjoyed a bit of company. He was used to being alone, though, so it didn't bother him.

He smiled at Robbie when the man came back into the kitchen. He hovered by the door, watching Cyril, and even though Cyril wanted to ask him what was on his mind, he didn't. He didn't want to spook Robbie any more than he already was.

Things had been tense with the three of them in the apartment. Robbie was afraid of Vale, which was puzzling, yet not. Cyril wasn't afraid of Vale because he knew how big Vale's heart was and that he'd never hurt anyone who didn't deserve it, but to Robbie, Vale was a professional killer who'd shot him. Vale was trying to fix things, but that was still Robbie's point of view, and Cyril didn't blame him.

"Are you all right?" Robbie asked.

"I've been better, but I'll be fine." As long as Vale came home. "You don't have to keep me company."

"I want to."

Cyril was surprised, but he gestured at a stool by the island. "Feel free to sit down."

Robbie did, looking like he was about to vault over the island to return to the living room. From where he was, Cyril had a good view of the couch, so they might be able to continue talking if he did, but he didn't think Robbie would be okay with that if he felt the need to run.

"Tell me about your job," Robbie eventually said.

"I thought you were afraid of it."

"Not afraid, more like—uncomfortable. I mean, I know necromancers exist, obviously, and I'm glad there was one at hand when I was killed, but knowing that I was dead and that I'm not any more kind of freaks me out."

"Would it freak you out if you'd died and someone had performed CPR on you?"

"Well, no, but it's not a bullet to the head."

"Does it matter? Either way, you'd be dead."

"I suppose it wouldn't. There was a *bullet in my head*, though."

"*Was* is the right word."

"And even though it's not there anymore, I still have a sign."

Unfortunately, there was nothing Cyril could do about that. For now, Robbie kept the hole covered with bandages, but eventually, he'd be able to go to a doctor to have it fixed. Cyril couldn't imagine it was easy to see it every day in the mirror. He wished he could heal physical wounds, but his ability only worked on the dead. Once they were alive, it was out of his hands.

"How do you do it?" Robbie asked.

"You mean, how can I be a necromancer or how I do my job?"

"Both, I guess."

"Well, I'm a necromancer because I was born one. I didn't have a choice. As for how I do the job, I'm not sure how to explain it. I can feel everyone's life force and their soul, I guess. When someone dies, I can use my ability to find their soul and pull it back."

"You make it sound easy."

"To me, it is. It's as easy as breathing, and I barely have to think about it."

"So bringing me back to life was easy?"

"It was, especially so because Vale was hurting over what

happened to you. He was worried he'd hurt an innocent person, and he was right. I wanted to soothe his pain, and the best way to do that was to bring you back."

"I don't think he cared that much."

Cyril put down his knife and fully faced Robbie. "I know you're wary of him, and I don't blame you. To you, he's the guy who shot you. You have to remember there's much more to him than that, though. He's a full human being, a human being I love. Yes, he kills people for a living, and a lot of people wouldn't be comfortable with that. Sometimes, I'm not, but I trust Vale. I know how his handler chooses his jobs, and I know that he doesn't hurt innocent people. He was lied to, which is why he killed you, but he's trying to fix that. I'm not saying you have to become his best friend, but at least give him a chance." At the very least, it might make things less awkward when we're all in the apartment.

"I'll try," Robbie offered. "For you. I can't thank you enough for what you're doing for me. If it wasn't for you, I'd be dead."

"You'd be dead if it wasn't for Vale, too. You don't have to become his best friend. Just stop actively leaving the room when he's there. You're going to hurt his feelings."

Robbie blinked. "Really?"

Cyril snickered. "Probably not. Still, he wants to get to the bottom of this, and you're involved, so maybe the two of you can work together."

"Maybe," Robbie murmured.

Cyril doubted that Robbie and Vale would get very far with their friendship, although he could hope. More importantly, he was glad that he and Robbie were building a friendship, because it would make living together easier, and, more than that, Cyril wanted more people in his life.

Getting into the building was ridiculously easy. Even some-one not as experienced as Vale and Russell would have managed it, so for them, it was a piece of cake. If Vale hadn't been so pissed at Peter West, he might have considered giving him tips to keep himself and his office more secure. As it was, he was ready to set it on fire himself if West didn't leave him alone.

Russell and Vale found West's office without any trouble. The secretary had left about an hour earlier—they'd kept an eye on her as she did so, and unless she returned, it meant that West was alone in his office. The door was slightly open, causing a ray of light to fall on the secretary's desk. It was neatly organized, with the pens parallel to the side of the desk. It was a bit *too* neat if you asked Vale, but no one had.

"Ready?" Russell asked in a whisper.

"I've never been more ready to do anything," Vale whispered back.

He didn't knock. He pushed open the door and strode into the office as if it was his. Peter West was on the phone, sitting behind his desk and smoking a cigar. Vale wrinkled his nose and forced himself not to tell West that smoking caused cancer. Frankly, if cancer took West, everyone would be better off.

"I'll have to call you back," West said without taking his focus off Russell and Vale.

He hung up his phone, put down his cigar, and grabbed a glass from his desk. He drank down whatever had been left in it and put it back down before getting to his feet. "I recognize you," he told Vale.

"Yeah? Do you recognize me because you hired me to kill your father, or is it because you hired other people to kill me?"

West's smile was sly. "I thought one of them would have gotten to you by now."

"I'm good at what I do, Mr. West."

"You are. It's a pity, really."

"What is? The fact that you thought you could have me killed or the fact that I'm good at my job?"

"Both. I don't anticipate having to eliminate anyone else, and you know too much, just like Robbie did, so unfortunately, you can't be allowed to live, no matter how good you are at what you do." West snorted softly. "I couldn't believe it had been that easy when I got the news from your handler that you killed him. I haven't seen his body, though, and as far as I know, his parents aren't organizing his funeral. What did you do?"

Vale grinned. "Wouldn't you like to know."

"I would, because I paid you to kill him."

"You also paid to have me killed, yet here I am. Things don't always work the way you want them to, do they?"

West stared at Vale. It gave Vale the creeps, but he didn't want West to know he was getting to him, so he kept his chin high and stared back.

"Why are you here?" West eventually asked.

"To ask you to take down the hit on my head. I'm not sure why you thought it was necessary to have me killed, but I'm a professional. I'm good at my job, as you pointed out earlier. Professional assassins who blabber end up dead sooner rather than later. I don't talk about my jobs, ever. I hadn't thought twice about you or your father until you sent me to kill Robbie."

"I want to believe you, but believing people brings bad things. I don't think I can afford to do that."

"You're not going to take down the job?" Vale hadn't actually expected him to. He hadn't wanted to go straight to the nuclear option, which was to kill West.

Vale didn't usually kill without someone hiring him to. It wasn't a hobby or something he enjoyed doing. It was a job, and he did the job he was hired to do. For West, he'd happily make an exception. He wanted the man dead, and not only for putting out a hit on his head. If West as much as looked in Cyril's direction, Vale would make sure he could never see again with those eyes. He would pluck them out and drop them to the ground before stomping on them.

Russell bumped his shoulder against Vale's. "You look murderous," he murmured.

"That's because I am." Vale straightened his back and squared his shoulders. "There aren't a thousand different ways out of this, West. Either you take down the hit and allow me to return to my life, or I kill you."

Vale wasn't surprised when West started laughing. The man was unhinged. Anyone in the business knew that you didn't kill professional killers. If you did, who would kill on your behalf? And Vale was one of the best. He did what he was hired to do without asking questions, and he left everyone satisfied — except the person he killed, but Rachel always checked who that person was. She had with Robbie, too, but there hadn't been much to find beyond where he'd worked.

Vale should have made the connection then, but he'd been so busy obsessing over Cyril and their relationship that he hadn't felt quite like himself recently. It had been a mistake, and now, he was here, threatening a man so he would take down the hit on his head. It was ridiculous, and he hated it.

"Just for that, I'll add another fifty thousand dollars to the job," West said, still sounding amused. "I won't take it down, not until you're dead, anyway." His gaze drifted to Russell, who'd thankfully been quiet the entire time. Vale wouldn't have been surprised if Russell had done a running commentary. "What about you? Do you need money?"

Russell crossed his arms over his chest and glared. "I'm not going to kill my best friend just because you're asking me to."

"Your best friend? That's interesting. I wouldn't have thought that professional assassins had friends."

"Just because you're a monster that no one can stand doesn't mean everyone else is," Vale snapped. "Since you're refusing to take the hit down, I'll have to do it another way."

West arched a brow. "By killing me?"

"You're not leaving me any choice, West." Vale had tried, but if West didn't want to listen to him, Vale would have to take care of things differently.

"There is no choice to make. The hit remains. I'm glad you visited before you got killed. This was . . . interesting."

Vale stepped forward, intent on hurting West the way West was hurting him. After all, West seemed to have a death wish, so no one would care if Vale killed him, right?

But Russell grabbed Vale's arm and dragged him toward the door. "You can't think there's no security here," he muttered. "They're going to strike when you least expect it, which means they'll probably do it while you're killing West. Get your head out of your ass, Roux."

"Shut up," Vale snapped, but Russell was right. He needed to think about this logically instead of allowing his heart to take over. This was his job, dammit. He might not be entirely sure what West's plan was, but he would find out, and he'd put an end to it.

And to West.

CHAPTER SEVEN

When Cyril's phone vibrated on the coffee table, he glared at it. The only people who would call him were his mother, Vale, and Russell. Since Vale and Russell were together, doing whatever it was that professional killers did when their colleagues were hunting them, Cyril hoped it was his mother, but he'd heard from her only this morning, and she wouldn't have a reason to call him again so soon unless something bad had happened, and he really hoped that wasn't the case.

"Are you going to answer that?" Robbie asked from the other side of the couch where he was petting Oscar.

Cyril sighed and grabbed the phone. "I think it's for a job."

"And why don't you want to answer?"

"Because I'm not sure I'm comfortable leaving the apartment without Vale. He's out right now, so I'm going to have to decline the job, and I never like doing that."

"You could go on your own. I mean, you and Vale haven't been together that long, right? What did you do before?"

"Well, my boyfriend wasn't being hunted by a bunch of professional assassins."

"I suppose that's true. You're not the one being hunted, though. That would be me and Vale."

"But someone might try to get to him through me. Besides, just because I'm a necromancer doesn't mean my life is never in danger."

"I suppose that's fair. What do you want to do, then? Because whoever's calling is going to hang up soon."

Cyril sighed and answered. He might as well tell whoever was trying to contact him that he wasn't available. "You're the necromancer?" the woman on the other side of the phone said.

"I am, but—"

"I need your help, please. I can pay you whatever you want."

"It's not a question of money, ma'am. I'm just not available right now."

Robbie patted Cyril's shoulder and pointed at himself. Cyril cocked his head, trying to understand what the man was saying. On the other side of the line, the woman was still begging and crying, and Cyril hated that he couldn't help her. He disliked refusing jobs, even when they couldn't pay him. This woman had mentioned that she could, but Cyril didn't care about that. No, he cared about not getting hurt and not getting Vale hurt.

"I'll go with you," Robbie offered.

That sounded like a bad idea because Robbie was supposed to be dead, but what was Cyril supposed to do? From what he could understand, the woman on the phone was saying that her granddaughter had fallen into the pool.

Cyril could never say no to kids. They didn't deserve to die so young, so when he could, he helped their families without requesting payment. It wasn't pleasant to reanimate the body of a child, but he had his ability for a reason. He wasn't going to hide from it, no matter how wary people were of him. He would use it for good, which apparently meant reanimating this child.

"Ma'am, please," he said. "I'll come. Can you text me the address?"

The woman sobbed. "Of course. I don't know how to thank you."

"If you found my number on my website, you know that I

can't make promises, so wait to thank me until we know it's going to work. I'll see you soon. Please, don't touch the body beyond pulling it out of the pool."

"We already did. She's so—she's never so still."

"I understand. Please text me the address."

The woman started crying, and Cyril felt close enough to tears himself that he knew he couldn't stay on the call. He quickly said goodbye and hung up, hoping he would get that text with the address.

"Why would you want to come with me?" he asked Robbie. "I know that my job makes you uncomfortable."

"Yeah, but you know what makes me even more uncomfortable? The thought of kids dying, especially when I know for a fact that you could save them."

"I probably can, but are you sure it's a good idea to come with me? There's a hit on your head."

"Not anymore." Robbie leaned down to put Oscar on the floor. "People think I'm dead. They're not going to come after me."

"If you're sure." Cyril hoped that Robbie was right and that no one would see him. In theory, no one should know where Robbie was, so they couldn't follow him, but there was always a chance that one of the assassins who were after Vale would be smarter than the others.

Cyril really hoped not.

"Fine. You can come." He might regret it, but he'd regret not helping that child more.

You would have thought he'd handed Robbie the moon. Robbie jumped to his feet and clapped his hands, way too enthusiastic. "I'm going to change."

Cyril watched him rush to the bathroom. He liked his apartment and spent as much time as possible there, but not everyone was like him. It was clear that having to hide was taking a toll on Robbie, so Cyril was glad he'd be able to help him. Hopefully, neither of them would end up regretting it.

Vale felt his phone vibrate in his pocket, but he and Russell were in a place where he couldn't answer. It could only be two people, and he really hoped that out of the two, it would be Rachel. If Cyril was trying to reach him, it meant something had happened.

It probably wasn't anything bad. Cyril knew that Vale and Russell were out, poking around places where professional assassins gathered. There were only a few in the city, and they needed information. Well, that was what Russell had said. Vale thought he had enough information to know what he needed to do.

Kill Peter West.

Normally, Vale wouldn't do this, but his life was in danger, and, even more importantly, Cyril's life might be. Peter West wouldn't take down the hit, even though Vale had asked nicely, and he wasn't a good person. All of that pointed to one solution.

Vale had to kill West.

"You're wearing your murder face again," Russell muttered. "Everyone's going to think you're up to something."

"That's because I *am* up to something." Which was thinking of as many ways as he could think of to kill West.

But Russell was right. It would be for the best if the people surrounding them didn't think he was planning something.

The bar wasn't full by any means. Two women were sitting at a table in the corner, sipping on drinks that were violently pink. A man was at the end of the bar, drinking what looked like water but probably wasn't. There was a group of four sitting at another table, talking in low voices. The bartender was scrubbing the counter, trying to make himself look busy.

Then there were Russell and Vale. They'd found a table

close to the bar, had ordered two beers, and had sat down.

"I'm not sure what you thought you were going to find here," Vale told Russell.

"I don't know. Mostly, information about who was stupid enough to take the hit on your head. Well, except Calypso. I don't think she's stupid."

"Why do you think she took it, then?"

"To be able to say that she was the one to kill you. That's not going to happen, but it would bring her a lot of fame and jobs."

That much was true. Vale had a reputation in their community. He'd been doing this job for years, and he'd been trained by one of the best. He also had quite a lot of hits under his belt, and he was known to work easily with others.

Including Calypso, who now wanted to kill him.

Someone slid into an empty chair at their table. Vale was instantly on high alert, exchanging glances with Russell before facing whoever was there. He recognized the man. In fact, he'd worked with him a few times.

"Heard you have a hit on your head," Whiskey drawled.

"Are you here to take the job?"

Whiskey snorted and snatched Russell's beer from Russell's hand. Russell made an indignant sound, but Whiskey just winked at him and took a sip.

The man was gorgeous. He looked more like a model than a professional assassin and was never afraid to use that to his advantage. He and Vale had had a thing once on one of the jobs they'd done together, but it hadn't lasted beyond a few fucks. They'd never even kissed, and Vale was happy to keep things that way. Still, he could enjoy watching Whiskey's soft blond hair and sparkling blue eyes.

"I'd never do that to you," Whiskey said. "But I heard that Calypso doesn't feel the same."

"She already warned me," Vale told him.

"Are you going to kill her before she kills you?"

"I'm actually hoping to be able to kill the client before anyone tries to do anything stupid."

Whiskey whistled. "Going straight to the source."

"I have to, when the asshole put a hit on me." Vale shook his head. "He hired me for a job a few years ago, and now he's cleaning up *loose ends*."

"Seriously? Does he really think we go around telling people what we do for a living and telling stories?"

"I don't know, and I don't care. He wants to kill me, and I want to stay alive."

"Well, it's not going to be easy, because Calypso isn't the only one coming after you. I've heard rumors about a couple of mercenaries."

"They're idiots," Russell muttered before snatching his beer back from Whiskey.

"I couldn't have said it better myself. They *are* idiots, but unfortunately, they're idiots with guns. You need to be careful, Roux. I enjoyed our time together too much to want to see you dead."

"I'm not planning to die," Vale reassured him.

Whiskey tapped his fingertips on the table, then leaned closer and murmured a few names in Vale's ear. Vale committed every single one of them to memory. "Thanks."

"No problem. I might not consider you a friend, but I respect you too much to let an asshole do this to you. I know a lot of us feel the same, but unfortunately, some *will* take the job."

Vale grinned. "And they'll regret it."

Whiskey laughed and clasped Vale's shoulder as he got up. "That's what I wanted to hear. I hope that the next time I see you, you'll still be alive."

Vale hoped for the same. He watched Whiskey walk away before turning back to Russell, who was staring at him.

"What?"

"You slept with him."

Vale snorted. "There was no sleeping involved."

"No way. He *is* who I think he is, isn't he?"

"I don't know. Who do you think he is?"

Vale had what he'd been looking for. He probably didn't have all the names of the people who'd decided to take the job, but he had some, so he knew who to look out for. It was a start, and hopefully, it would be enough to keep him safe until he could kill West.

He got to his feet, Russell quickly following.

"That was Whiskey, right?" Russell asked.

"I don't understand why you're so awestruck by him. You literally do the same job as he does."

"But I've heard things."

"So? He's just a guy."

Vale waited until they were out of the bar to take his phone out. Just like he'd thought, it was Cyril who'd called him earlier. He had a few missed calls and texts that explained that Cyril and Robbie had gone out on a job and shouldn't be home late.

Shit. Vale was supposed to be with Cyril when he went on jobs. He was supposed to protect him when he was working.

"He'll be fine," Russell said as he knocked their shoulders together.

"I know he will. Stop reading my texts."

"They're right there! Cyril said he didn't go out alone, so I wouldn't worry too much if I were you."

"He went out with *Robbie*. Do you really think Robbie can help in any way if someone attacks them?"

Russell grimaced. "Okay, you might be right."

Vale knew he was, but he couldn't just follow Cyril around all day, every day. He didn't think anything would happen, and if something did, Cyril would call him.

In the meantime, he might as well head home.

Cyril leaned away from the little girl. She was coughing and panicking, and he'd learned a while ago that when he reanimated kids, he needed to get out of the way as quickly as possible so that the child and their parents could reunite.

The girl's mother pushed past him, almost toppling him to the ground. She sobbed as she wrapped her arms around her daughter, pulling her into her arms.

A hand on his shoulder surprised Cyril. He smiled up at Robbie, and when Robbie offered him a hand, he took it and allowed the man to pull him to his feet.

They were in the backyard, next to the pool where the little girl had drowned. When Cyril and Robbie had arrived, everyone present at what looked like a small party was crying desperately. The woman who'd called—apparently, the girl's grandmother—had rushed him to the child, even though Cyril had assured her that with such a recent death, he had plenty of time. He understood why the grandmother had wanted him to reanimate the kid as quickly as possible, though.

The scene had been awful, but then, it always was when children were involved. The mother had been slumped next to her daughter, crying desperately, making a sound that Cyril had heard before but that always burned itself into his brain. It was the sound of a grief so deep that the person experiencing it couldn't make sense of it or process it.

But that grief was gone. Cyril had reanimated the girl, and she'd been reunited with her mother.

"That was incredible," Robbie murmured.

"It's my job."

"I still feel a little weird about it, but what you did for that girl was incredible."

Cyril opened his mouth to tell him again that it had just been his job, but someone pulled him backward, and he found himself engulfed in a pair of arms.

"Thank you," the grandmother sobbed. "I don't know how to thank you. I don't have a lot of money, but I'll give you everything I have."

Cyril was already shaking his head and hugging her back. "Don't worry about that. I'm just glad I could save her."

As far as Cyril was concerned, the satisfaction of feeling the little girl breathe again and watching her reunite with her mother was enough payment. These weren't the kind of people he wanted money from.

He was glad he'd dragged Robbie along because Robbie took charge of the weeping woman. He got her to sit down with the other members of her family, gently talked to her and her daughter for a few moments, then returned to Cyril's side.

Cyril wanted to go home. He was tired, and he wanted to see Vale. He was pretty sure he was pouting because when Robbie reached him, he rolled his eyes.

"I gave her your information because she insisted that she would at least bake you cookies to thank you, and I thought that you shouldn't say no to cookies."

"You thought right. That's the only form of payment I'd accept if I could."

Robbie nodded. "She and the girl's mother thank you. I'm pretty sure you're going to be flooded with baked goods, but I guess that's fine. Are you ready to go home?"

Cyril's phone vibrated in his pocket, and he quickly took it out. It was a text from Vale telling him that he'd seen Cyril's text and that he and Russell were almost home. He also told Cyril to be careful, and Cyril could almost feel the love Vale felt for him through the screen.

"Yeah, you're definitely ready to go home," Robbie teased as he guided Cyril toward the front of the house.

"Wait, my bag," Cyril said.

"As long as I can just throw everything into the bag, I'll get it for you. You go sit in the car."

"Yeah, you don't have to be too careful. Thank you."

Robbie nodded and went back, and for a moment, Cyril watched him walk away.

Working with him was surprisingly easy. He made dealing with the grieving family members easier, and Cyril enjoyed having someone to talk to. He knew this wasn't what Robbie wanted to do for the rest of his life, but he wondered if maybe if he got another call for a job, Robbie would want to go with him—as long as the body Cyril had to reanimate wasn't too far gone. Cyril wouldn't ask Robbie to come along if it was.

But they'd worked well together. Cyril had been able to focus on reanimating the little girl from the beginning instead of talking to the family. Robbie had kept everyone calm and away from Cyril, including the girl's mother. Cyril wouldn't have been able to do all of that on his own.

Maybe that was something to mention to Robbie once he wasn't running for his life anymore. Maybe, even though he was wary of Cyril and downright terrified of Vale, he wouldn't mind helping a necromancer.

Cyril could always dream.

CHAPTER EIGHT

Cyril liked Robbie, even with all the complications that came with him.

Robbie was still wary of Vale and tended to stay away from him when Vale was home, which wasn't that often these days. Cyril missed his boyfriend, but he wanted him alive, which was what Vale was working toward, so Cyril couldn't complain.

He wasn't lonely. He seldom was, even before Vale had entered his life, but things were different now. With Robbie hanging around the apartment and keeping him company, Cyril felt safer and less like he was drifting the way he had before meeting Vale and Russell. He figured that while he'd always be a loner at heart, meeting them had changed him. Now, he wanted to spend time with people. It couldn't be with his favorite person, since Vale had stuff to do, but Robbie was nice, and Cyril thought he could call him a friend, if not now, soon.

He glanced into the kitchen. Robbie was standing at the stove because he'd insisted on cooking lunch, and while Cyril had told him he didn't need to, Robbie's expression had been set, and he'd mentioned that with everything Cyril was doing for him, it was the least he could do. It didn't matter how many times Cyril told him that he wasn't doing anything most people wouldn't do, he still insisted he needed to thank him, and since Cyril didn't particularly enjoy cooking, he'd agreed. If Robbie wanted to cook for him every day while he was here, that was fine with Cyril.

He tapped on his phone, checking the time and resisting the urge to open social media. Lately, he'd only been taking the jobs he absolutely couldn't refuse, which left him a lot of time at home. Usually, he read, spent time with Oscar, and now, with Robbie, but there were only so many times he could do all of that before getting bored. He'd tried watching TV, but that hadn't lasted long, either, so a lot of the time he found himself mindlessly scrolling down social media and wasting time. He hated the feeling, but Vale wanted him to stay home. If that was what Vale needed to feel comfortable, Cyril was happy to give it to him. It made sense that Vale wanted to know that Cyril was safe and Cyril was fine staying home a bit more often than he had before.

He just hoped it wouldn't last forever. He wanted to help people, and while he was used to being on his own, it had never felt the way it did now, almost like he was a prisoner in his own life. He suspected it was because usually, *he* made the choice to stay home, but now, that choice had been made for him.

Something fell in the kitchen, making him jump. He twisted again to check in on Robbie, who appeared flustered. "Is there anything I can do?" Cyril called out.

"No. I have everything under control."

It didn't sound like it, but Cyril didn't push. He thought it was important for Robbie to be independent since his life had been taken from him. Cyril couldn't imagine what that felt like. Robbie had been trying to do the right thing, and because of that, he'd lost everything—his apartment, his job, his family. He couldn't contact any of them, not even to tell them that he was okay, because it was too dangerous. Just like Cyril could be used against Vale, Robbie's family could be used against him. If Peter West found out that Robbie was alive, he might send someone to grab them, and that was something everyone wanted to avoid.

"I'm never going to be a chef," Robbie said in a self-deprecating voice as he stepped into the living room. "Honestly, I thought I could manage more than grilled cheese, but I suppose it'll have to do."

Cyril smiled at him. "Grilled cheese is perfect."

"Wait until you've tasted it. I almost set it on fire."

He offered Cyril the plate he'd been carrying, and Cyril took it with a smile. If he was honest, the grilled cheese looked good. It was a little too brown, but nothing that would make eating it impossible.

"I guess that's one thing I can take off my list," Robbie said as he returned with a second plate and flopped on the couch. "I don't know what I'm going to do once this is over. I'll need to find another job, but I can't exactly explain what happened."

Cyril swallowed and licked his lips. He'd been thinking about that, but he was hesitant to share with Robbie. What if Robbie said no? Cyril wouldn't blame him since he was still afraid of Vale and wary of Cyril being a necromancer. He'd helped when Cyril had reanimated the little girl, but that didn't mean he wanted to stay on permanently. He probably wished he could go back to his life, his friends and the people he actually cared about instead of being stuck here with Cyril.

"You don't have to eat it if you don't want to," Robbie said as he reached for the plate.

Cyril pulled it against his chest. "I want to eat it."

"Are you sure? Because you look like you were wondering if I'd notice you throwing it in that potted plant."

"I'd never throw anything in Marsha," Cyril said, offended.

Robbie snickered. "It's adorable that you give your plants names."

"They're alive, so why shouldn't I?"

"Indeed, why shouldn't you?"

Cyril stared for a moment before shaking his head. "Sometimes, I don't understand you."

"Sometimes I don't understand myself, so it makes sense."

"What job do you want to do once you return to your normal life?" Cyril asked as he munched on his grilled cheese.

"I don't know. Clearly, Peter West isn't going to give me references, so it's not going to be easy. I like being someone's assistant, though. I like helping people."

"You're good at it," Cyril murmured. "You could find another job as a personal assistant."

"As long as they don't check my references, I guess."

"Or with someone who already knows you."

That was as far as Cyril got before the door opened. Robbie tensed, and Cyril half expected him to rush to the kitchen when Vale and Russell came in. Robbie had been working on his instinct to run from them, though. Cyril suspected that the fact that Russell was a dork helped a lot, which might be why Russell was spending so much time with them. Part of it was no doubt that he wanted to help his best friend, but he was a sweet man, and there was no way he hadn't noticed that Robbie felt more comfortable with him around, but then, Russell hadn't shot him in the head.

"Hey," Vale said with a smile as he rushed to Cyril's side.

Russell made a retching sound. "God, you two are so sickly sweet."

Vale turned to glare at him. "You're just jealous because I have a boyfriend."

"Hell yeah, I'm jealous. I want someone like Cyril, too."

"I'm sure you'll find them," Cyril quickly reassured him. He didn't miss the way Robbie and Russell glanced at each other, and the sight made him grin. Maybe he could find more than one way to convince Robbie to stick around.

"I can make more food," Robbie offered.

Vale shook his head. "Why don't you sit down?"

Robbie flopped back down onto the couch and stared. "That doesn't sound good."

Vale's expression was grim. "That's because it's not."

Vale hated to be the one to erase the smile from Cyril's lips, but he didn't have a choice. He and Russell had been poking around these past few days, looking into the situation and getting more names of people who might come after him, and they hadn't found anything good. Cyril and Robbie needed to be prepared, just in case.

Russell leaned over and stole half of Robbie's grilled cheese from his plate. He ignored Robbie's glare and took a bite, humming as he chewed.

Vale looked away from Russell's weird flirting and focused on his boyfriend. "We already knew that Peter West wouldn't take down the hit, so it's not a surprise that it's still up."

"He's offering even more money now," Russell said gleefully. "Vale isn't a record yet, but I think that if he continues bothering West, he might become one."

Vale scowled at him. Was it really necessary to scare his boyfriend even more? Russell seemed to understand Vale even though he hadn't said a word.

He shrugged. "What? He should know."

"I don't want you to hide anything from me," Cyril said. "If something's going on, I want to know, just in case."

Even though it was what Vale had planned, hearing it from Cyril's lips made him want to scream. He needed to protect his boyfriend, dammit. How was he supposed to do that with a bunch of assassins coming after him?

"I'll be fine," Cyril reassured him. "Eventually. I know I wouldn't be able to do anything against a professional assassin, but so far, things have been okay, and it's not like I'm their target, anyway."

"Some of these guys are ruthless and won't hesitate to hurt you if it means hurting me," Vale said.

If he thought Cyril would be scared, he should've known better. Cyril's jaw set, and he raised his chin as if challenging Vale. "Let them come. I'll kick their asses."

"More like you'll throw Oscar at their heads," Russell commented.

He was almost done with his grilled cheese and turned puppy eyes to Robbie, who quickly stuffed the rest of his half into his mouth. It was like watching a car crash. Vale could have told Russell that starting anything with Robbie was a bad idea, but honestly, he wasn't sure it was. Robbie was being hunted — or rather, he would be hunted if people found out he was alive — and probably needed a distraction. There was no way he could return to his old life once all of this was over, and maybe being with Russell would make him feel better about himself and his chances of getting a normal life back.

As if that was something that could exist in the same world as Russell.

If Robbie ended up with Russell, his life would be anything but normal. Not a lot of people were ready to deal with that. On the other hand, people like Vale would rather die than have to live what most people considered a normal life. Being a professional assassin had brought him a lot of trouble, but he wouldn't have it any other way. Besides, it had also brought him Cyril, and he could never be sorry for that.

"We have a list of names of people we think are going to come after me," he told Cyril. "The most dangerous is definitely Calypso. She's been a professional assassin for twenty years, starting when she was only fifteen or so."

"That's awful," Robbie said.

Vale nodded because it was. Calypso hadn't gotten into this line of work because she wanted to. She'd been molded into what she was now, which was one of the things that made her so dangerous. "There are also a bunch of mercenaries and other assassins, so we'll have to be careful, but Russell and I can deal with it."

"I don't want either of you to get hurt," Cyril said because he was too nice for his own good.

"Someone is going to get hurt anyway. I can't allow any of these people to get to me."

"Of course not. I just wish Peter West would take down the hit and realize this isn't the right thing to do."

There was no way the man would do that, but Cyril didn't know him.

To be fair, neither did Vale, but he sure knew him better than Cyril, and he knew that nothing he could do or say would convince West to take down the hit. West was afraid that Vale would talk about what had happened with his father, which was ridiculous, but Vale doubted he could change West's mind.

He'd tried, and it hadn't worked.

"I think there's realistically only one way to deal with West," Vale said. "I know you don't like the thought of me doing this, but I'll have to kill him."

He expected Cyril to agree, even though he wouldn't like it, and Robbie to have something to say about it. He wouldn't blame him. For most people, the thought of killing someone in cold blood was atrocious and not something they were willing to consider.

But Robbie nodded, and Vale found himself staring at him and trying to understand.

"I agree," Robbie said.

"You do?" Vale asked.

Robbie rolled his eyes. "I thought you'd be happy considering everything. Yeah, I think you should kill him. He had his father killed, and he tried to kill me." Robbie grimaced. "Well, he did kill me. The only reason I'm not dead is Cyril. I know West, Vale. Once he gets his teeth into something, he's like a dog. He won't let go until he's forced to, and I don't see another way to make that happen. I want to be free of West and this mess. I want to go back to my normal life, and if killing West is the only way to do that, I'm all for it."

"And it's not like you have a choice, since he won't take down the hit," Cyril added. "You tried doing this the right way. You can't force him to do anything, and he's never going to stop coming after you. I agree with Robbie. You need to kill him."

Vale and Russell exchanged a glance. That hadn't gone the way they'd expected. In fact, it had gone completely different, so much so that it was hard to believe. Vale wasn't going to try to change Cyril and Robbie's minds, though.

He nodded. "I'll kill him."

CHAPTER NINE

"I'm going crazy," Robbie declared as he stared at the ceiling from where he was stretched out on the couch.

Cyril was amused. "We could go to the grocery store," he offered.

Robbie glanced at him. "And have Russell look at me like I betrayed him?"

"You wouldn't be betraying him. You'd be going to the grocery store. We can grab a few things, maybe cook dinner for when Russell and Vale return."

Robbie sighed heavily and turned back toward the ceiling. "I can't believe this is my life. I can't believe that going to the grocery store sounds fun." He threw his hands in the air, almost dislodging Oscar from his chest. "Is this what my life is going to be from now on?"

"You know it won't be for too long. Once West has been dealt with, you won't have to hide anymore because no one will care if you're alive or dead." Cyril sucked in a breath. That wasn't a great way to say what he'd been trying to say. "You know what I mean."

Robbie snickered. "I do. My parents will be happy to find out I'm not dead in a ditch somewhere. They're probably worried."

Cyril thought of his mother and how she'd react if he were in Robbie's position. He hated the thought, but there was nothing they could do. Hopefully, having Robbie return to them healthy and safe would soothe the pain they were feeling now.

"You should call them," a woman said, startling both Robbie and Cyril.

For a second, they stared at each other. Robbie stretched out on the couch, Cyril curled up in the armchair. Then, they both jumped to their feet. Robbie clutched Oscar against his chest as he bumped into Cyril's side. Together, they faced the woman who'd just spoken.

Cyril didn't have to ask her name to know who she was. Vale had described Calypso, and she was just as Cyril had imagined. Hell, she was even more beautiful than he'd thought anyone could be. Her long blonde hair was loose, her lips were red, and she looked amused. She was tall, yet she was wearing heels. It didn't seem sensible for a professional assassin, and Cyril hoped it meant she wasn't here to kill him and Robbie.

Shit. Robbie was supposed to be dead. Maybe Calypso was here for him, or maybe she was here for Vale but would decide to kill Robbie, too.

Cyril stepped forward and placed himself in front of Robbie. Robbie made a strangled sound, and Calypso's smile widened.

"You're cute. I can see why Roux fell for you," she said.

"What do you want?" Cyril asked. He tried to keep his voice steady, but he wasn't sure he succeeded.

She waved. "I'm not here for either of you, although this is interesting," she said as she grinned at Robbie. "Aren't you supposed to be dead? I'm sure I saw your face on the forum."

"Forum?" Robbie asked as if he wasn't sure he wanted to find out what she was talking about.

"Where people request the hits," Cyril said without looking back. "It's how Artemis chooses the jobs for Roux and Brutus."

"Oh."

Calypso's smile widened. She didn't look dangerous like

this, but Vale had said she was lethal, so she had to be. She looked around. "I know he's not home."

"Please, leave him alone," Cyril begged. "You're colleagues. He told me that usually, professional assassins don't take hits against each other. I don't know why you felt you had to take this one, but please."

Calypso stared at him for a moment. "You know, you're not wrong. Usually, we don't kill each other. It's bad for business."

"Killing him *will* be bad for business." Cyril disliked Vale's code name, and he couldn't bring himself to say it again. It was a part of Vale he barely knew, a part he didn't *want* to get to know. He didn't hate Vale for the work he did, and he could even understand it in a way, but he didn't want to be involved.

Not beyond reanimating Vale's targets, anyway.

"You're not wrong," Calypso said slowly. She eyed Cyril up and down, and he wondered what she would ask of him in exchange. He was sure she *would* ask for something. It was in the way her gaze sparkled, and from the little Cyril knew about her, she wouldn't be one to miss an opportunity like this.

Cyril was one of the best necromancers in the city. It was counterintuitive to think that a professional assassin might need him for anything, but they both dealt with death in their own way, and he'd already proved useful to Vale.

"All right," she said. "I'll let Vale live. I can't make promises for the others who decide to come after him, though."

"You don't have to."

"But you owe me a favor."

Robbie grabbed Cyril's arm and squeezed, but Cyril couldn't look back. He couldn't allow anyone to distract him. "All right," he agreed.

"What are you doing?" Robbie whispered angrily.

Cyril continued staring at Calypso. "I'll reanimate one person for you, but that's it. That's the favor."

Calypso tapped her chin with a finger. "A life for a life. I like that."

When Vale got a notification on his phone, he didn't think much of it until he saw it came from the app of the security system he'd installed in the apartment. As soon as he saw that one of the cameras had detected something, he started freaking out. He quickly opened the app and watched in horror as Calypso climbed up to one of the windows, glanced at the camera, and waved. She slid the window open and disappeared inside.

"We have to go," he told Russell as he grabbed his arm and pulled him away from the bar in which they'd been about to enter.

"I haven't even had a beer yet," Russell complained.

"You'll never have a beer again if you don't follow me and help me kick Calypso's ass."

Russell became all business. "Where is she?"

"At the apartment. I saw her on camera."

Russell nodded as if that was all he needed, and it probably was. All thoughts of beer had been abandoned. He was focused on keeping Robbie and Cyril safe.

Vale wanted to drive, but he knew it would be safer if Russell did. He was too frantic at the thought of something happening to his boyfriend. They needed to get back to the apartment as soon as they could, and burning red lights and risking the cops stopping them wasn't the best way to make that happen. Wrapping the car around a pole also wasn't. If Vale wanted to save Cyril, he needed to keep his calm and focus on what he could do instead of freaking out about what might happen.

He bounced his knee as Russell drove them through the city. He kept an eye on the app on his phone, but he hadn't put cameras inside the apartment. He hadn't wanted to take away what little privacy Cyril had, and now, he regretted it. There was no way for him to know what Calypso was doing.

A few minutes later, he saw her leaving through the front door. The door slammed shut behind her, which had to be a sign that Robbie and Cyril were all right. At the very least, one of them was able to slam the door shut. That meant they were fine, didn't it?

Vale didn't even wait for Russell to park the car. He was out as soon as the car was in front of the building, rushing for the stairs. He didn't see Calypso anywhere, not even when he threw open the front door and made both Cyril and Robbie jump.

The two of them had been huddled on the couch, but as soon as Vale walked in, Cyril rushed to him. He threw himself into Vale's arms, and Vale wrapped himself around him, hugging him close as he looked around the apartment.

"She's gone." Robbie looked happy to be able to say that.

"Are you sure? She could be hiding somewhere."

"I don't think she is. I spied on her through the window, and I saw her climb into a car and drive away."

Vale nodded, knowing that Russell would be poking around the building and making sure Calypso wasn't there. Vale would have to check that the apartment was clear, too, but it could wait a moment since Robbie and Cyril agreed that Calypso wasn't here anymore.

He looked down at his boyfriend, who was still pressed against him. "What happened? Did she hurt you?"

Cyril shook his head. "We're both fine. She didn't touch us."

"What did she say?"

"She was here for you."

77

"Cyril made a pact with her," Robbie blurted out.

Vale sucked in a breath. "A pact? What pact? What's Robbie talking about?"

Cyril grimaced and put some space between them, which didn't make Vale happy. "I begged her not to hurt you. I told her that killing you would be bad for business, and she agreed. She said she wouldn't accept the job as long as I owed her a favor."

Vale groaned. "That's not good, Cyril. God knows what she's going to ask of you."

"I told her I would owe her one reanimation. That's it."

"And she said yes?"

"I don't think she actually wanted to hurt you. I think that initially, she was amused by the situation, and she decided to see what would happen. She seems nice."

Vale snorted. He loved that Cyril saw the best in everyone, but in this case, it wasn't something he could get away with. Calypso wasn't a nice person. Vale didn't think any of them were. They killed people for a living. They'd killed their humanity a long time ago, especially those who'd been groomed into the position. Vale was one of the lucky ones. He'd fallen into this job through the military, and he'd always had his eyes wide open. He'd known what he was doing, but some of these assassins had been way too young when they'd been forced into this life, like Calypso.

He'd do his best to shield Cyril from all of this. Cyril's heart was too soft, and he would never understand some of the things Vale had done. They weren't a secret, but Vale couldn't deny he was afraid of how his boyfriend would react if he found out about some of the stuff in his past.

He pulled Cyril closer and kissed the top of his head. "All right. I guess I should be relieved that she's not coming after me anymore. Don't make any more pacts with assassins, though."

Cyril shook his head and pushed closer. "I promise I won't. She looked nice, but she was kind of scary."

"She's both those things. She's beautiful, but she's also lethal." It was a miracle that she hadn't hurt Cyril and Robbie. She'd been hunting Vale, and normally, she would do anything to get to her target. The fact that she hadn't used Cyril made Vale wonder if maybe he'd misjudged her.

Whatever the case, this mess was almost over. This had been one step too far. Vale wouldn't allow anyone to hurt or scare Cyril.

It was time to kill West.

CHAPTER TEN

"I really don't think this is a good idea," Cyril said.
He looked from Russell to Robbie, wondering if either of them were listening to him. He couldn't make the choice for them, but he didn't like any part of this plan.

"Russell knows what he's doing, babe," Vale said. "He wouldn't have offered to take Robbie back to his apartment if he wasn't sure he could get both of them out of there quickly if anything happened. I know you've never seen him work, but I promise you that they'll be fine."

"But it's dangerous. West could have sent people to Robbie's apartment, or maybe one of the assassins from that forum is looking for him. Calypso knows he's alive."

"She made a deal with you."

"So she wouldn't kill *you*. I never mentioned Robbie in that deal."

And now, Robbie wanted to go home. Well, he wasn't planning to move back into his apartment, but he wanted to pick up a few things, which Cyril could understand. Not only had Robbie been killed and reanimated, but he'd also been stuck in an apartment that didn't belong to him with people he didn't know. He didn't have any of his things beyond what he'd had at the hotel where Vale had killed him, and that hadn't been much. Everything had fit into a backpack, and Robbie had been borrowing clothes from Cyril.

"We'll be fine," Russell reassured Cyril. He leaned forward and patted Cyril's knee. "I promise we'll be careful and that I'll keep an eye on Robbie. No one will get to him."

"I'm also worried about you."

Russell's smile was easy. "I'm touched, but you don't have to be. I don't think Calypso would have told anyone that Robbie's still alive. It's none of her business. She didn't take the hit on him, and she didn't order it, so she has nothing to win or lose by keeping her mouth shut. West probably doesn't know that Robbie's alive, either. I don't think he would've checked into it. He's the kind of guy who orders people around and assumes that everyone will do his bidding. Besides, Robbie's been staying in the apartment since Vale killed him. No one would think to look for him here."

"But they *would* think to look for him in his apartment."

"We'll just go in and out," Russell promised. "I'll bring him back in one piece, and we'll both be safe. You have to trust that I can do my job, Cyril."

Cyril sighed. "It's not that I don't trust you to do your job."

"You're nervous and worried. I get it, but you don't have any reason to be. I've been doing this for years."

Cyril wouldn't win. Robbie had batted his lashes at Russell, and Russell had jumped to do what he wanted. It would've been funny if Cyril hadn't been so worried. There was nothing he could do about this. Robbie and Russell were going, and that was that.

Vale wrapped an arm around Cyril's shoulders and pulled him close. They were on the couch while Russell was sitting in the armchair. Robbie hovered next to the door as if ready to bolt as soon as Cyril said he could. He wasn't waiting for Cyril's approval, but it was clear that what Cyril thought mattered to him.

It was touching. Cyril hadn't thought he and Robbie would become friends, especially with how wary Robbie had been of him initially, but he'd hoped they might anyway.

He wanted Robbie to feel at home in the apartment, even though it would be hard. The place was too small for all three of them, especially with how much time Russell was spending there. Cyril wouldn't have it any other way. He had very few friends, and he wanted all of them close. He was especially worried about Robbie, but he couldn't lock him up and wait for all of this to blow over. It wouldn't be fair to Robbie.

He sighed. "Fine. I won't stop you from going, but know I'll worry about you the entire time."

Russell grinned. "Is that a threat?"

"No. What *is* a threat is that I'll send Vale after you if you don't come back in a few hours."

Russell's eyes twinkled. "Oh, I'm so scared."

Vale looked unamused. "You should be. You know I'll do anything in my power to make Cyril happy, and he won't be happy if something happens to you and Robbie. You better come back, and soon."

Russell was still smiling, but Cyril could see the determination in his gaze as he nodded. "Don't worry too much. We'll be back so quickly that you won't even realize we're gone."

"I highly doubt that." Vale's arm around Cyril's shoulders tightened. "Cyril and I will take advantage of this time alone."

"I did *not* need to hear that," Robbie muttered. "But please, don't do it on the couch. I sleep there."

"How about the coffee table?" Vale teased.

Cyril's cheeks flushed. He wasn't used to this kind of banter, but then, he wasn't used to having friends. Joking around about sex made him uncomfortable, but it was on him.

Russell got to his feet. "We'll be home soon," he promised.

Cyril was pleased that Russell considered his apartment home, although if he was going to start spending more time here, Cyril might have to look into a bigger place. He didn't want to because he loved his apartment and because Robbie would probably find another place eventually, but for now, they were all stuck here.

Russell and Robbie left the apartment, and Cyril stared at the door. He wanted to go with them, but at the same time, he couldn't imagine putting himself in danger like that. The one time he'd been kidnapped had been more than enough for him.

"They'll be fine," Vale promised as he cuddled Cyril close. "I know that Russell doesn't act serious, but I promise that he knows what he's doing. He wouldn't have offered to take Robbie back to his place if he didn't think he could defend him if something happens."

Cyril sighed. "I know. I'm not worried because I think Russell won't be able to defend Robbie. I don't want anything to happen to either of them. They're my friends."

"I should never have introduced you to Russell," Vale grumbled.

His tone made Cyril smile. "You love him."

"I wouldn't be too sure about that." Vale's smile turned into something heated. "But I do love you. How about we take advantage of the time alone?"

Cyril's mouth went dry. "That's fine with me, but not on the couch."

Vale blinked, then groaned. "Dammit."

Cyril was a lot more relaxed by the time Vale was done with him. Vale had wanted to stay in bed, but Cyril had made him dress and dragged him back to the living room so they would be there when Robbie and Russell returned. Vale had been annoyed, but when the door flew open, and Robbie walked in with red eyes and tears rolling down his cheeks, he knew that his boyfriend had been right to want to be there.

Cyril was on his feet in seconds, rushing toward Robbie. Vale was surprised to see that Robbie didn't hesitate to throw himself into Cyril's arms. He might have been wary of him initially because Cyril was a necromancer, but the two of them had been spending a lot of time together, and that wariness seemed to have gone right out the window. Robbie needed a friend and a shoulder to cry on, and Cyril was willing to provide that.

Vale got up and went to help Russell haul in the few bags Robbie had brought along. "How did it go?" he asked, keeping his voice soft so he wouldn't disturb Robbie.

Russell grimaced. "There wasn't anyone waiting for us there or anything like that, but it's clear that Robbie's family has been looking for him. One of them left a message on his kitchen table, and he's been crying since he saw it."

That explained the tears. "Do you know how much they know?"

"I have no clue, but he wants to call them."

"Absolutely not. It's too dangerous."

"I should be able to choose if I want to do this," Robbie said as he sniffed. "I understand how dangerous it is. I even understand it's dangerous for you and Cyril, so if you want, I'll leave and go to another hotel. I need to call my family, though."

"What are you going to tell them?"

Robbie hesitated. "I won't go into details. I don't want to put them in danger, but I need them to know I'm okay and that I'm protected. I know that I've been keeping my distance from you, and I can't say I'm really comfortable being close to you, but I trust you to keep me safe until this mess is over and I can go home. I won't tell them anything."

"Please," Cyril said. "He needs to do this. Think about his family. They deserve to know he's alive."

Those two were going to be the death of Vale, but he didn't even care. Cyril had asked for this, and Vale would give Cyril whatever he wanted. "Fine," he said. "But you have to be careful about what you say. Don't tell them why you had to run or that you were killed. Don't say anything about the re-animation or where you are. Don't mention West at all, or Cyril and me."

"That's not going to leave him a lot of things to say," Russell pointed out.

Vale glared at him. "Do I look like I care? They don't need to know where he is or what happened. They just need to know he's okay, so he doesn't need to give them any details."

"I promise I won't," Robbie quickly said. "I don't want West to get to them. I just want them to know I'm not dead."

"Russell will stay with you, just in case."

"I don't need a babysitter."

"No, but you do need a bodyguard. Someone's trying to kill you, remember?"

Robbie scowled. "Someone did kill me."

"And I'm really sorry about that."

Russell leaned closer to talk to Robbie, and Vale turned his attention to his boyfriend. "I really hope we're not going to regret this."

"I don't think we will. He doesn't want to put them in danger. He just wants to reassure them."

"I can understand that, but they're going to want to know what happened and where he is, and he's going to feel compelled to tell them because they're his family, and he loves them."

Sometimes Vale was glad he didn't have anyone left. His parents had been older when they'd had him, and he'd been an only child like both of them. He didn't have any family left. He only had Rachel and Russell, and now, Cyril.

And maybe Robbie. The jury was still out on that, but Vale suspected that with how close Robbie and Cyril had become, Robbie would be a permanent fixture in his life. It wasn't a bad thing, although Vale wished that Robbie could forgive him for shooting him. Maybe he would, eventually. In the meantime, Vale would do what he could to keep Robbie safe. It was the least he could do for him, but even more so, it was something he wanted to do for Cyril.

Vale would do anything to keep his boyfriend happy, and if that meant protecting Robbie from West and Robbie himself, he'd do it.

CHAPTER ELEVEN

Clearly, the security system Vale and Russell had put up at the apartment wasn't enough to keep people away. Calypso had snuck in without even trying to hide, and while she was one of the best, Vale wouldn't put it past other assassins who were considering killing him to do the same. They wouldn't be as nice as Calypso had been, and they might hurt Cyril, which meant that Vale was done waiting.

He couldn't waste any more time. He had to take out West, and he had to do it as soon as possible. Once West was gone, so would the hit on Vale's head. With no one paying to kill him, Cyril would be safe.

Vale had to believe that.

He thought about what his next step would be as he went for a run around the neighborhood. He didn't go far, even though Russell was with Robbie and Cyril. He was wearing sunglasses and a hat, just in case, because he didn't want anyone to recognize him, but he didn't expect anyone to get to him.

He should've known better.

Calypso was one of the best, but she wasn't the only good assassin out there. Vale had hoped that most of them would stay away from the hit, but there were more than a few who had a grudge against him, so it wasn't a surprise to see that at least one of them had decided to try to get rid of him and get paid to do so.

He was running past a small alley between two buildings when something caught his arm. He got pulled into the alley, losing his balance and slamming against the wall. He reacted on instinct, the way he'd been trained. When a punch came toward his face, he ducked, grinning at the sound of bone hitting brick. The man who'd grabbed him swore, but Vale was already moving.

He grabbed the man's waist and turned them around until he could slam the guy against the wall. He grabbed the man's head and slammed it against the bricks, hearing another crunching sound. The man yelled and tried to push Vale away, but Vale had already reached behind his back and grabbed his gun. He didn't hesitate before shooting the man between the eyes, just like he had Robbie.

But he wouldn't reanimate the assassin.

He was a bit out of breath as the man slid to the ground, but that had more to do with his run than with what had just happened. Vale waited to see if anyone had heard anything, but the alley was quiet. He always used a silencer, but this was the middle of the day, so someone might have heard something.

Nothing happened, and no one came to ask what was going on. He couldn't hear sirens. He was pretty sure no one had noticed anything, but that still left him with a dead body.

He poked at the man with his foot and took out his phone. He wasn't worried about the dead body. He dealt with them all the time.

"I thought you'd forgotten about me," Artemis said when she answered.

This was a work call, even though Vale wasn't working. "I have a body for you."

She swore. "What happened?"

"Guy attacked me while I was on a run. We're in an alley, and I don't think anyone saw us, but the sooner you can have the cleaners here, the better."

"I've just sent them a message. I also sent them your

location so they'll know where to find the body. They said it would be about twenty minutes."

"I'll hide him behind the dumpsters. That way, even if someone peeks in, they won't see him."

"I'll make sure the cleaners know where to look. What happened?"

"I'm going to guess this is one of the assassins who decided to take the hit on my head."

"That didn't do him much good. You have his name?"

"Give me a second."

Vale stuck his phone into his pocket without hanging up, grabbed the dead man under the armpits, and dragged him toward the dumpster. He made sure the body was hidden from the main street, then patted the guy down to find his wallet. Most assassins wouldn't walk around with identifications, not real ones anyway, but it always came in handy to have a fake ID in case the police stopped you. Vale did the same, so he wasn't surprised to find what he'd been looking for.

"ID says that his name is James Brown." Vale snorted. "Looks nothing like the singer."

"What happened to creativity?" Artemis muttered. "It's a known alias, though. The guy's code name was Diablo."

That sounded familiar, but it wasn't anyone Vale had worked with. Not that it would've changed anything. If someone attacked him, he'd defend himself, no matter who they were. He just hoped he wouldn't have to kill anyone he was friendly with. "Well, you can tell his handler that he's gone."

"I'll do that as soon as I have the cleaners' confirmation that they got him. You're all right?"

"Never better, but I should go home. Cyril's going to freak if he doesn't see me soon. He's been all over the place lately."

"Can you blame him?"

"Not at all, which is why I'm headed home."

"I'll let you know when the cleaners are done."

Vale hung up, made sure the body wasn't visible from the main street and ran home. This wasn't how he'd thought his run would go, dammit.

He didn't have time to start sweating again before he got to the apartment. He went in, ignored Russell and Robbie, who stretched out on the couch watching TV, and went to the kitchen to grab some water. It was just his luck that Cyril was there, sipping on some tea and reading on his phone.

He looked up when he heard Vale, and Vale couldn't help but smile at him. If this was what he'd come home to every day for the rest of his life, he'd die happy.

But Cyril's eyes widened, and he rushed forward. "What happened? Are you okay?"

Vale blinked. "I'm fine. Why are you asking?"

"Because there's blood on your shirt."

Vale swore and looked down. Sure enough, there was blood on his shirt. "Dammit. It's one of my favorites."

"Who cares about your shirt? What happened? Whose blood is that?"

"Not mine. Someone attacked me while I was coming home. You don't have to worry, because I took care of him."

"That's not going to stop me from worrying. What did he want?"

"To kill me. I already called Artemis, and she confirmed he was an assassin."

Cyril had been pale before, but it was nothing next to how pale he was now. Vale hugged him, and while he wished there was more he could do to reassure him, he was useless. Assassins would continue to come for him until the hit was taken down, and while West was alive, that wouldn't happen. In the meantime, Vale would have to deal with any assassin who came at him.

That wasn't going to be fun.

Cyril was freaking out, and he was pretty sure Vale knew it. He didn't want his boyfriend to worry about him when it was clear that he needed to worry about himself, so he did his best to school his expression. At the same time, he couldn't stop running his hands over Vale's arms to check that he really was fine.

"You can't leave the house again," he said.

"That's going to be hard, since I have things to do," Vale said with an indulgent smile.

"Russell can do whatever you need to do. I'm not letting you out of my sight."

"What does Russell have to do?" Russell asked as he walked into the kitchen.

"For one, Russell has to stop talking about himself in the third person," Vale muttered. "It's creepy."

Russell grinned. "Why would Russell want to do that? Russell likes annoying Vale."

Even though he was worried and freaking out, Cyril smiled at the banter. When he'd first met Russell, he hadn't realized how close he and Vale were. Now, he was part of their family, and he couldn't imagine it any other way.

"I got attacked on my way back," Vale said, getting through the banter. "Diablo."

Russell wrinkled his nose. "The guy really thought he could get you? I mean, he had some experience, but I worked with him once, and he was sloppy."

"He's not going to be sloppy anymore. I left his body behind a dumpster."

Cyril shuddered and pushed closer to Vale. He didn't care that his boyfriend had just been for a run and that he was sweaty or that there was blood on his shirt. He just needed to be as close as possible.

Luckily, Vale didn't seem to have a problem with that. He wrapped an arm around Cyril's waist and held him close as he and Russell talked.

"You called Artemis?" Russell asked.

"Yeah, she got the cleaners to pick up the body. She'll let me know when they're done."

Russell nodded. "Good. That's the second one now, though. We need to do something. Diablo wasn't dangerous, but Calypso is, and it's a miracle that she walked away. I don't think anyone else will."

Vale had told Cyril that most of the good assassins wouldn't take the hit, and Cyril hoped that was true. Calypso had been the exception, and it looked like Vale had defended himself easily enough from this Diablo, but Cyril didn't want to risk it. What happened if Vale was distracted or if the assassin was lucky? Cyril couldn't allow anything to happen to Vale.

Vale sighed. "Why don't you go grab something for dinner? I'll shower, and we can sit down and eat and decide what to do next," he told Russell.

"We're finally moving?"

"I don't think we have a choice."

Cyril didn't like any of this. He was terrified to lose Vale and, with him, everyone else. He didn't want to be alone again. He loved his mother, but he wanted more. He wanted Vale and Russell, Robbie and Rachel. He wanted his friends, and most of all, he needed his boyfriend to be all right.

"Well, whatever you decide to do, you know I'll be there."

Vale pushed Russell. "Then go get me something to eat."

Russell pouted. "Russell isn't happy. Russell wants some love."

"Russell will get his ass kicked. Get out of my apartment."

Russell laughed and obeyed. Cyril heard him stop in the living room to talk to Robbie, but he was more focused on

Vale. He gingerly touched one of the drops of blood on Vale's shirt, relieved to know it didn't belong to his boyfriend but worried anyway.

"I'll be fine," Vale promised.

So far, he had been. He'd been attacked, but from what Cyril could see, there was barely a scratch on him. That didn't mean he'd be so lucky a second time. The best way to ensure that nothing happened to Vale was to take down the hit on his head.

Cyril wished that West was a reasonable man. Vale and Russell had already tried talking to him, and unfortunately, West wouldn't change his mind. Cyril wasn't surprised. He tried to stay away from people like West, but in his job, he didn't always succeed. He despised them — the people who thought they were so powerful and rich that nothing mattered but them, the people who thought they were better than anyone else just because they'd been born into wealth. To West, Vale didn't matter. He'd been a weapon to have his father killed, nothing more, nothing less. Now, he wanted to get rid of that weapon, to throw it away. He hadn't counted on Vale fighting his way out of this mess, but he was, and he was dragging Robbie with him.

Cyril was sure that Artemis would eventually find something that would keep West away from Vale. The problem was that they didn't have time. This was only the first attack, but it wouldn't be the last, and Vale might not be as lucky next time.

"I should go shower," Vale said gently.

"I'll come with you." There was no way Cyril could allow him out of his sight. He was still freaking out, and it wouldn't get better if he had to stay away from his boyfriend. He was being clingy, which was something he'd wanted to avoid, but he thought these were extenuating circumstances. Surely, Vale understood.

Cyril was always worried that he was too much for Vale, but once again, his boyfriend reassured him with nothing more than a glance. He smiled and nodded, and when he stepped away, he took Cyril's hand and pulled him toward the bathroom. He understood, even when Cyril didn't have the words to explain or when he thought he was too much and that no one in their right mind would want to deal with him.

Vale always did.

"Russell said he'd be back in twenty minutes," Robbie called out. "No funny business in the bathroom. I shower there."

"It's too late for that," Vale called out, snickering when Robbie made retching sounds.

Robbie might still not be sure what to make of Vale, but to Cyril, it looked more and more like they were building a relationship similar to the relationship between Vale and Russell. Cyril was an only child, but he'd seen this kind of banter between siblings.

He hoped they would keep it up, even after this mess was over. Vale might have never said he was lonely, and maybe he wasn't, but he had led a lonely life, just like Cyril. They might be fine with that, but maybe it was time for both of them to welcome people in.

But the next time, it would be great if they made a friend Vale didn't kill first.

Vale felt better now that he was clean. At the very least, he wasn't bloody anymore. The way Cyril had freaked out over it had made Vale feel like shit because he never wanted Cyril to be that scared again. Cyril deserved to be happy and not have to worry about people killing him or his boyfriend. That might be a problem considering Vale's job, but it was too late for Vale to take a step back. He loved Cyril, and he was too selfish to leave him.

Which meant he'd have to change things. Retirement was an option he'd considered before, and he couldn't avoid it anymore. He'd thought that maybe he could make it work by taking fewer jobs, but he was starting to realize that the best thing for Cyril would be for him to quit entirely. The problem was that he didn't have any idea what he would do if he wasn't an assassin. He'd already asked Rachel to look into it, but between one thing and another, he still didn't know what his options were.

And he wasn't about to find out. He had other things to focus on, like keeping Cyril and the people he cared about safe.

He glanced at Cyril and Robbie, who were huddled together on the couch, watching something on Cyril's phone. Robbie cackled, and Cyril's cheeks flushed, which made Vale wonder what they were watching. He wanted to ask, but it was none of his business. If Cyril wanted him to know, he'd tell him.

It was good to see Cyril with Robbie. Vale had been worried because he didn't know Robbie and didn't want a stranger to invade his personal space, but he'd felt guilty because he'd killed Robbie, and he'd never been able to say no to Cyril when he wanted something. Things had ended up going well. Cyril had made a friend, and while Vale still worried about him all the time, at least he didn't have to worry that Cyril was lonely.

The front door opened, and Vale tensed even though he doubted any of the assassins who took the job to kill him would walk in through the front door.

"I'm back," Russell announced.

"It was about time," Vale called back.

Russell walked in with a bunch of bags. "If you're that

hungry, you should've come with me. I already ate my fries."

"As long as you didn't eat mine."

Russell put the bags on the coffee table and flopped on the floor. Oscar, who'd been hiding under the couch, made a bee-line for him, climbing onto his lap in a clickety of bony tentacles. Russell had never been afraid of Oscar, but Vale still wasn't sure what to think of the pet. Was it bad that Oscar creeped him out?

It wasn't even because Vale didn't understand how Oscar worked. He had no idea how Cyril had managed to give him life, especially since he was made up of a bunch of bones that came from different animals and a skull, but that didn't matter. He was freaked out by the fact that Oscar's body was a human skull. Every time he looked at Oscar, his empty sockets stared at him.

But Oscar was a sweet pet. Cyril loved him immensely, so Vale wasn't about to ask him to get rid of the thing. Besides, he was pretty sure if he tried, Oscar would haunt him and try to kill him.

Russell patted the top of Oscar's body and pulled things out of the bags. Robbie and Cyril started helping him, and Vale smiled at his boyfriend when Cyril handed him a burger. For a moment, the only sound in the room was them eating. Unfortunately, the silence gave Vale too much time to think.

One of the assassins had found him. That wasn't a surprise. In fact, he'd expected it to happen. If it had just been Diablo, Vale wouldn't have been worried, but he knew that behind that one man was a long line of mercenaries and assassins who wanted his head, if anything, for the money.

"You have your murder face on again," Russell commented as he stole a fry from Vale and stuffed it into his mouth.

Vale glared at him without heat. "I was thinking about what happened today."

Robbie wrinkled his nose. "I don't want any details. I'm eating."

"And I've already heard too many details already," Cyril said softly.

Vale was sitting in the armchair, so he couldn't hug his boyfriend. Instead, he knocked their knees together, smiling when Cyril looked up at him. Cyril smiled back, and for a moment, everything was right in Vale's world. Who cared if he had to retire? He'd been an assassin for years, and maybe it was time for him to stop and focus on his personal life. He didn't have one before, but now that he had Cyril, he wanted to spend as much time with him as he could. Being an assassin who worked all over the country wasn't conducive to that.

Vale had no doubt that trouble would find him anyway, even if he wasn't a working assassin. That was how things went. Most of them didn't retire. Usually, they died, sometimes on a job, sometimes in other circumstances. Vale didn't want that to be his end. He wanted to die an old man holding Cyril's hand.

"Have you heard from Rachel?" Russell asked.

Vale nodded. "The body was taken away, so we won't have to worry about that. It doesn't look like anyone noticed anything."

"That's good. The last thing you need is for someone to see you killing the guy."

"Yeah. I don't know how Diablo's handler took the news. He still hadn't responded when Rachel called."

"What's our next step, then? Because they're going to keep coming. We could keep you in the apartment, but Calypso got in, and I'm pretty sure that at least a few of the people coming after you will try to blow up the entire block to get you."

"I think that the only thing we can do is go straight to the source."

Russell bounced a bit, dislodging Oscar, who slowly

turned his head toward him in a way that made Vale shudder in horror. Russell didn't seem to mind, because he patted Oscar's head again until Oscar settled back down.

"We're going to kill West," Russell declared.

"You knew this was the plan all along."

"Well, yeah, but I know you. You're trying to be nice for your boyfriend."

Cyril gaped. "What do you mean?"

"We already decided that we need to kill West, but he still hasn't done anything about it," Russell pointed out. "That's because even though he wants to kill the guy so he can be free, he knows you're not comfortable with all of this, so he's been waiting."

"You can't wait until I'm comfortable," Cyril said. "Besides, we already talked about it. I told you I understood that it was the only way for you to survive. If I have to choose between you and him, you're always going to win."

Vale had known that, but it was so nice to hear it from Cyril. He was important to Cyril.

Russell clapped his hands like the idiot he was. "It's show time."

CHAPTER TWELVE

It wasn't show time. Vale was ready to kill West, but it would be impossible to do if they didn't find the guy first. He and Russell had gone back to the office, but West hadn't been there. They'd poked around a bit and asked Rachel for help, but apparently West had gone on vacation, and no one had seen him in almost a week. Vale wondered if their little visit to the guy had scared him. It hadn't looked like it at the time, but it certainly did now.

That was a problem.

If they didn't know where to find West, they couldn't kill him. If they couldn't kill him, the hit on Vale's head was never coming down.

That was a problem, too.

Vale had been staying in the apartment to avoid a repeat of what had happened the last time he'd been out, but he was slowly going nuts. He was ready to climb the walls, and unfortunately, it was becoming a problem for Robbie and Cyril, too.

Vale had never done well stuck inside. He didn't mind staying home when he had Cyril, but eventually, he had to go out. He wanted to go for a run or get ice cream or food. Hell, he'd even take the grocery store over staying in the apartment. As happy as he was to be with Cyril, as much as he liked the tiny space, the walls were closing in on him, and he was going to start screaming if nothing changed.

He almost cheered when his phone vibrated on the coffee table. Robbie rolled his eyes when Vale snatched it up and got to his feet from where he was sitting on the floor. He'd been leaning against Cyril's legs as they watched TV, but he hadn't been focused on whatever was on the screen.

"Hey," he said when he answered after checking who the caller was.

"I swear that the next time you get yourself in this kind of trouble, you're going to pay me to do all this research," Rachel said.

She sounded both annoyed and smug, which gave Vale a thrill. "You found him."

"Damn right, I found him. It wasn't even that hard. I just had to check all of his properties, and he has dozens."

"So he's hiding."

"I don't know about that. Some people would call it a vacation, but *I'd* call it hiding. He didn't go far, though. Apparently he owns several buildings in the city. He also owns a house."

"That's where he is." It wasn't a question, because it made sense. If West wanted to hide, he was going to try to stay away from as many people as possible, which wouldn't be easy living in an apartment.

"It certainly looks like it. The house is pretty isolated. It's not really in the city, but on the outskirts, and it's extensive. From what I was able to find, there's a wooded area all around the house. There's also a very expensive security system."

"But you'll help us through it."

"Of course I will. You bring in too much money for me to want you to die."

Vale smiled fondly. He knew Rachel couldn't care less about the money. She wanted Vale to be okay because they were friends. She was his handler, so she got paid every time he finished a job, but that wasn't what linked them. They'd be friends even after Vale retired.

He hadn't yet found an opportunity to tell Rachel that he was planning to, and she'd be a bit confused and worried, but they'd work something out.

As soon as Peter West was dead.

"Send me the coordinates," he told Rachel.

"Already done. It should be in your inbox. You'll let me know when you're planning on going?"

The front door slammed open, making Vale, Robbie, and Cyril jump. Robbie also squeaked and scrambled to grab a pillow from the couch and place it in front of him as if it would defend him from whatever was coming in.

Russell stepped into the apartment. He was grinning like a loon, maybe because he had a man swung over his shoulder. Vale could only see the man's legs and the ass, so he had no idea who he was. He looked unconscious, though.

Or dead.

"Look what I found," Russell declared loudly, closing the door with his foot and dumping the man to the floor.

The man's head lolled to the side. There were no holes in his forehead, so he was probably still alive. Vale couldn't see any blood anywhere.

"What the fuck?" Robbie screeched. "Who is that? Why did you bring him here?"

Russell raised his hands as if to calm down Robbie. "He's an assassin. I found him lurking around and decided that Vale and I could threaten him a little, just for old times' sake. It's been a while since I threatened a baby assassin."

Robbie gaped. "A baby assassin?"

"This guy can't be more than twenty-five, if even that," Russell said as he gestured at the unconscious man. "I mean, he might have started early like Calypso, but that's not how things usually go. He's brand-new."

Vale was still on the phone with Rachel, so he quickly explained what had happened as he crouched next to the man.

"See if you can find his name," Rachel said, sounding annoyed.

"I'll let you know who it is."

"And if I need to send the cleaners."

Vale hesitated. It would be safer if he killed the guy, but was that what he wanted to do? Considering how young the man was, he probably had no idea who Vale was. He'd seen the hit, had decided he needed the money, and accepted it. He wouldn't have expected the situation to be so complicated.

Neither had Vale.

"I'll give you all the details," he promised Rachel. "As long as *you* give me all the details I'll need to get to West."

"Like I said, it's already in your inbox. I hope you're still alive tomorrow, Vale."

"It would be inconvenient if I weren't."

Vale hung up. He poked at the man's cheek with his finger, grinning when the man groaned and started blinking rapidly.

"Artemis found West," Vale told Russell, looking up.

Russell looked like a golden retriever who'd found something precious and brought it back to their master. It was a miracle he wasn't bouncing, but from the way his body vibrated, he was excited—or he expected to be told he was a good boy, which wasn't something Vale was willing to do with Russell of all people.

"When are we going?" Russell asked.

Even though they'd been friends for years, it still gave Vale a thrill that Russell had planned to go with him, whatever happened. It would have been easy for him to take that back, but instead, he'd volunteered to come along without Vale having to ask. They bickered all the time, and Russell was annoying, but they were brothers.

"Let's take care of this guy first, then we can go," Vale said.

Vale didn't have a plan, but he didn't really want to kill the kid. He grinned when Oscar slid out from under the couch and climbed onto the man's chest. He was so close to the man's face that he was the first thing the man saw when he opened his eyes.

He screamed and passed out again.

"This is annoying," Russell said.

"Let's see if we can find his name," Vale said with a sigh. He gently lifted Oscar, handed him off to Russell, and patted the man down. He found his ID—no doubt fake, but at least he'd have a name to call the guy. "John Smith." He snorted. "Really?"

"Well, he does look like a John Smith," Russell said. "A bit boring and definitely an idiot."

Vale jostled John. His eyes fluttered open, and for a second, John stared at Vale.

He finally seemed to remember Oscar and quickly scrambled into a sitting position. He looked around wildly, his focus stopping on Russell, who was cuddling Oscar while staring at John and smiling a very creepy smile. It made him look like a villain from a movie.

"You shouldn't have come," Russell said dramatically. "Now you'll be my minion for the rest of your life."

The man squeaked and looked around for an exit, but there was nothing. He really was a baby assassin, and Vale felt kind of sorry for him. He couldn't have known what he was getting into when he'd decided to take the job.

"Go," Vale told him. "And don't accept jobs that involve killing another assassin. That's not how we do things."

The man's blue eyes were wide. He nodded as if he was afraid Vale would give him to Oscar to eat if he didn't agree as quickly as humanly possible. Russell pouted, but Vale opened the door. He didn't help John up from the floor, but he didn't need to. John was out the door in seconds.

Vale slammed the door shut and turned. Russell was still pouting, but having Oscar in his arms seemed to soothe him.

Vale quickly rubbed the top of Oscar's head. Maybe he wasn't so bad after all. It certainly had been funny when John had fainted because Oscar had been there.

"That was a thing that happened," Robbie said slowly. He cocked his head. "What the fuck just happened?"

"We had a little visitor and got answers from Rachel. She knows where West is."

Cyril was worried. He knew this was necessary so Vale could stop hiding and Robbie could return to a more or less normal life, but he couldn't help but wonder if it was the right thing to do.

He didn't care about West. He didn't care if the man died after he'd put a hit on Vale's head. No, he was worried about something happening to Vale and Russell, who would be going into the house to find Weston and kill him. Cyril didn't know much about West, but he did know that the guy was a powerful and rich asshole. That meant security systems and guards, which in turn meant more possibilities for Vale and Russell to get hurt.

"We should go now," Vale said. "The sooner we end this, the better it will be for everyone."

"Everyone but West," Robbie added.

Vale pointed his finger at him. "I like how you think."

Those two had been bickering until half an hour ago. Now, they were bonding over murder.

What had Cyril's life become?

He wouldn't have it any other way. Hopefully, once West was gone, they could settle down and be happy. He didn't want to have to think about people dying for a long time.

Unfortunately, that wouldn't be possible with his job, but at least he wouldn't have to worry about someone he cared about dying. Right now, that was all he could think about.

"You can't just barge in and start shooting," Russell said. "As fun as that sounds, we need to do at least a little planning."

"But I wanted to surprise him."

Vale wasn't pouting, but Cyril was pretty sure it was a close thing. It would've been funny in other circumstances.

Russell and Vale squeezed on the couch between Robbie and Cyril, and Vale opened his email. Cyril was plastered against his side, but he didn't mind. He leaned harder against his boyfriend, smiling as Vale and Russell started talking.

It took Cyril a moment to realize that something was bothering him. Vale and Russell were planning on going there, but when they spoke, it was clear they were going alone. There were no mentions of Cyril or Robbie.

It wasn't like Cyril wanted to kill West himself. Even if he'd been tempted, it just wasn't something he thought he could do. He didn't kill people. He reanimated them.

But that didn't mean he wanted to be left at home to worry about what would happen to Vale. What if something did and Vale never came home? How was Cyril supposed to find out if he wasn't there? Besides, they were in this together. Cyril might not have the first clue about how to fight, but they were a team, and that mattered to him.

"Robbie and I will come with you," he declared.

Vale snapped his mouth shut before opening it again. "What?"

"You heard me. Robbie and I are coming."

"I'm not," Robbie said. "I'm fine waiting here, where I'll be safe."

"What if something happens to them and they don't come home?"

"Why do you think we wouldn't come home?" Russell asked. "We're good at what we do, some of the best assassins in the forums. We'll be working together, which means we'll be even better."

"I don't think that's how it works," Robbie muttered.

Cyril turned his full attention to Vale. "Please. I understand it's dangerous and that you want to protect me, but I want to protect you, too. I won't be able to do anything during the fight, but I can wait for you outside and take care of you if you're wounded."

"I'll be fine," Vale said.

"Maybe so, but we're coming anyway. We're a team. Where you go, I go."

"I'm not part of this team, so I'll be waiting here on this nice couch," Robbie said.

Cyril glared at him. He needed Robbie to support him the way he'd supported Robbie. Thankfully, he only had to stare a few moments for Robbie's shoulders to slump. "Fine. I want to go, too."

Vale groaned. "This is a bad idea."

It probably was, but Cyril couldn't care less. Where Vale went, he went. He would probably be uncomfortable on most of Vale's jobs, but Cyril wasn't willing to compromise.

He knew what he wanted, and what he wanted was to keep Vale alive. If there was even one thing he could do to make it so, he'd do it.

No matter the consequences.

Vale didn't want Cyril anywhere near West or the place where West was. He supposed he could order his boyfriend to stay home, but the set jaw and mulish expression on Cyril's face told him he wouldn't win this fight. Cyril would find a way to come, no matter what.

"It's dangerous," Vale told Cyril. "You're a great necromancer, but you don't know how to fight or how to defend yourself. I won't put you or Robbie in danger. Russell and I know how to do our jobs, and we'll be in and out before you can even start worrying."

"No. I trust that you know how to do your job, but I want to be close." He hesitated. "That way, if something happens to you, I can reanimate you as quickly as possible."

That hadn't yet crossed Vale's mind. "You'd reanimate me if I died?"

"Unless you don't want me to."

"Of course I want you to. I want to spend the rest of my life with you."

"Which is why I'm coming."

Vale opened his mouth to say *no fucking way*, but Russell cleared his throat.

"He's going to come anyway," he pointed out. "He and Robbie will just take the car and follow. We might as well allow both of them to come with us. At least we'll know where we left them and how safe they are."

Cyril had never been so happy as he'd been since he'd met Vale, and he hated Peter West for putting a wrench into that. He hated him for putting Vale in danger.

Vale pinched the bridge of his nose. "I guess you should come, then," he said, not sounding one bit happy. "But you'll stay outside. Hell, you'll stay in the van so that no one can see you."

Cyril frowned. "We have a van?"

"We will when we go there. You promise you'll stay out of sight?"

"I'm certainly not planning on entering the house with you. Why would I?"

Vale stared at him like he was nuts. Maybe he was, a little. After all, he was willingly throwing himself into danger. This wasn't something he would've done before, but he really couldn't let Vale go on his own.

"I don't know. Why are you so intent on coming if you

don't know what you'll do there?"

"I want to be close in case something happens to you or Russell, but it doesn't mean I have to see West or where he sleeps. I'll stay out of harm's way in the van with Robbie. We won't try to come in, and we'll wait until you're back before even thinking about doing anything. I just think it's safer for you two if I'm close by."

"Fine," Vale said with a heavy sigh. "I suppose you can come. You're an adult, and I can't forbid you to do anything."

Cyril was a little hurt by that. "And you don't need my skills?"

"Well, I hope you'll never have to use them on me. I don't want to die, Cyril. I certainly don't want you to have to reanimate me after I do. No one should have to go through that."

"I still want to stay home," Robbie interrupted.

"You're coming with me," Cyril told him. "I'm not doing this on my own."

"And you chose me to go with you. Lucky me."

Cyril was the lucky one. He'd found love and friends, and he was going to cling to all of it with both hands so they couldn't be taken from him. If that meant going with Vale to wherever he was going to kill West, he'd do so with a smile.

CHAPTER THIRTEEN

Vale stared at the house in front of him. He hadn't expected anything else from Peter West. The place was massive, but considering how few guards they'd seen, there was a good chance it wasn't as well protected as it should be. That would go to Vale's advantage.

The house looked like a white box. It was all harsh angles, something Vale didn't appreciate. It didn't look comfortable or welcoming. It looked expensive, and it looked like Vale would break something if he breathed too hard.

"What do we know?" Russell murmured.

He was sitting in the passenger seat of the van. He'd been the one to find the thing, and Vale was tempted to complain about the fast-food smell that lingered, but he didn't. Russell had come through, like always, and he was here with Vale when he didn't have to be.

Vale looked down at his phone. Rachel had emailed him every detail she could find about this house, from when West had bought it to what changes he'd made inside. "There's a panic room."

Russell swore. "Of course the asshole has a panic room."

"He's probably been locked in there since he arrived. How many guards did you count?"

"Just the two, but there could be more. There should be."

If West was smart, there would be more. This place was too big to have just two guards, even with a panic room in which West could hide if something happened. "Let me text Rachel. She's been checking the cameras, so she'll know more."

She knew where they were and what they were about to do, so she answered right away. It felt like they were on a job. Vale supposed they kind of were, even though no one would be paying him to kill West.

His satisfaction would be enough.

West had crossed a line. Not only had he threatened Vale and sent people after him, but Cyril had ended up in the cross-hairs. Calypso hadn't done anything to him, but she could have, just like any of the other mercenaries and assassins who decided to take the job. That wasn't something Vale could accept.

His phone vibrated. He looked down to find a string of texts Rachel had sent him. "Okay, she said that she counted six guards in total."

Russell snorted and leaned forward. "Is West stupid, or is he so attached to his money that he won't pay more guards to protect him?"

"I don't know, and I don't care. It's going to make our life easier."

"I'm ready when you are."

Vale nodded and texted Rachel back. "She'll tell us if West heads to his panic room. She has eyes on the inside so she can guide us," Vale explained as he twisted lightly in his seat.

Cyril and Robbie were huddled in the back of the van. Robbie looked like he'd rather be anywhere but here, which Vale knew was the case because he'd complained multiple times about being forced to come with Cyril. Cyril's eyes were wide as he stared at Vale, and Vale half expected him to find a reason not to let him leave. He wasn't sure what he would do if Cyril asked him not to do this, but thankfully, he wouldn't have to find out.

Cyril didn't try to stop him. He listened to Vale explain what he and Russell would do, and when Vale slipped in the earbud that would allow him to hear Rachel as she guided him to West, he leaned closer.

"Be safe," he ordered.

Vale reached back and lightly cupped his hand around the back of Cyril's head. "I promise I will be," he murmured before kissing his boyfriend.

"Now go out there and do what you have to do. Robbie and I will be waiting for you here when you return."

That was the main thing that spurred Vale to move. He was doing this to protect his boyfriend and to give Cyril a happy life that he couldn't have if West was hunting them.

Vale and Russell slid out of the van. Vale texted Rachel one last time before tucking away his phone and taking out his gun.

"Hello, boys," Rachel's voice said through the earbud. "There are two guards outside, four inside. West is in the kitchen."

"Guide us," Vale ordered.

He and Russell fell into an easy rhythm. It wasn't the first time they'd worked together, and as always, it was as if they could read each other's minds. That was one of the reasons the two of them were so close. No matter how annoying Russell was, he was damn good at his job, and Vale trusted him with his life. The fact that they were in sync also helped.

They snuck onto the property and moved toward the house. Rachel's voice was steady in their ear, telling them when to stop when to move forward, and when to wait. She warned them when the first guard reached them, and since Russell lightly tapped Vale's shoulder, Vale let him take care of the problem.

"The second guard is coming from your left," Rachel warned.

Vale tucked himself around the corner and waited. When the man appeared, he allowed him to continue walking for a moment before stepping behind him. He didn't hesitate. He grabbed the man's head with both hands and twisted.

The man's body dropped. Vale grabbed him and dragged him toward the wall, moving him around the corner so that people wouldn't see him from inside the house. Once he was done, he checked in on Russell, who'd done the same thing and was waiting for him.

They continued moving. Rachel guided them toward the safest entrance and unlocked the door from where she was. She also took care of the security system, cursing at how simple and easy to attack it was. Vale was glad because it meant their job would be easier. West had more money than sense, but then, that was often the case.

They finally got inside the house. Vale could hear people talking, but he kept his focus on what Rachel was telling him since she had eyes on them. "There are two guards with him," Rachel said. "Another one is in another part of the house, possibly where they're sleeping because it looks plain. I can't see the fourth guard, but there aren't any cameras in the bedrooms. I'll keep an eye open in case he pops out of somewhere."

This wasn't going to be easy. West would see them as soon as they stepped into the kitchen. They'd have to take care of the two guards before they could get to West, which would give West the time to hide.

Unfortunately, there wasn't another way to do this. Vale and Russell glanced at each other. Vale gestured that he'd take the guard on the left, and Russell nodded, a sign he'd take the one on the right. Neither of them could take care of West until they killed the guards. They just had to hope that West would be too startled to move. Rachel hadn't mentioned him being armed, but that wasn't what Vale was afraid of. West wasn't the kind of guy who killed people. No, he was the kind of guy who hired professional killers to kill an assassin.

He was going to regret it.

"I have to get out of this van," Robbie said as he scrambled for the back door.

Russell and Vale had only left five minutes ago and those five minutes had been heavy. The silence in the van had made Cyril want to scream. Instead, he'd pressed his lips together and had waited, just like he'd promised Vale.

"We said that we'd stay here," he said as he tried to stop Robbie by grabbing his arm.

Robbie shook off his hand. "I shouldn't be here. This man tried to have me killed. Hell, he *did* have me killed. I died, and it was all because of him. What do you think he's going to do if he finds me here?"

"He won't find you," Cyril tried to reassure Robbie. "He's inside, surrounded by guards. He's not going to come out here to find you."

"You can't know that."

"West mainly cares about himself. It wouldn't be safe for him to come out here for you, so he's not going to do it."

Robbie threw his hands in the air. "He doesn't have to. He can send someone to do the dirty work for him."

He threw open the doors and stepped out. Cyril hesitated for a moment, torn between his promise to Vale and his friend. He didn't want to leave Robbie alone, though, so he quickly followed him, only to find him pacing by the van. It was a relief to see he wasn't running all the way back to the apartment.

"This was a stupid idea," Robbie said as he raked a hand through his hair. He got his fingers stuck and glared. "You and I shouldn't be here. We should have stayed at home, where we would've been safe. Why did you insist we come along? You're not going to be able to do anything for Vale and

Russell. They're in there, and you're here. If one of them gets killed, you'll have to go inside that house, and if you do, Peter West will hurt you."

Robbie was terrified, which wasn't a surprise. Cyril wished there was more he could do for him, but beyond offering him a safe place to stay and being his friend, he couldn't think of anything.

"Staying at the apartment would have been just as dangerous," he said, pointing out. "What if West had sent someone to kill you there? Without Russell and Vale, you wouldn't have been able to defend yourself."

"But I don't want to be here. This is dangerous. It's stupid."

"I have to agree with that," a voice drawled.

Robbie squeaked and turned in the direction of the voice. Cyril was slower, swallowing as he saw the guard pointing his gun at them.

Where had he come from? Did his presence here mean that Vale and Russell were in trouble? Even if it didn't, Robbie and Cyril definitely were.

"We're not doing anything wrong," he quickly said.

The guard turned his attention to him. "You mentioned my boss. That means you're not here just because you have a flat." He gestured at the van. "Open the door wider."

He wanted to see what was inside. Cyril moved slowly, frantically thinking about a way for them to get out of this. Vale was going to be so pissed when he found out. He was going to kill this guard, even though, for now, the man hadn't done anything but threaten them with a gun, which was his job.

Cyril pushed open the van doors and stepped aside so the guard could see in. There was a flash of movement in the periphery of Cyril's vision, and he turned just in time to watch Robbie plonk a thick branch on the guard's head.

The guard didn't stand a chance. He went down like a sack

of potatoes, his gun sliding in front of him. For a moment, Cyril and Robbie stared at each other. "You hit him with a tree," Cyril said.

Robbie dropped the branch and stepped away from it as if it was about to attack him. "It's a branch."

Cyril eyed the gun. He'd never touched one, not even one of Vale's, and he hated that he was going to have to start today. Still, he gingerly picked it up, holding it with two fingers as he retreated toward the van.

"What are you doing?" Robbie asked as he followed. "It's dangerous. Put it down."

"I will, but not next to the guard. He'd just use it against us."

"You're going to shoot yourself."

There was a strong possibility of that happening, so Cyril pushed the gun under the van. When he turned, he saw that Robbie was looking at him like he was nuts.

"What? That way, the guard won't know where I hid it. He can't reach it easily, either."

"I guess it's better than holding it." Robbie swallowed. "Do you think I killed him?"

His expression told Cyril that if he had, he'd regret it. He'd been defending himself and Cyril, but that didn't mean he'd wanted to kill anyone.

"I'll check," Cyril said gently.

Robbie nodded and followed Cyril back to the guard. The man was face down in the dirt, and he was heavier than Cyril expected, so he and Robbie had to work together to get the guard on his back. Cyril winced when the guard's head hit the ground a bit too harshly when he landed on his back, but he quickly checked the man's pulse because Robbie was still staring at him.

"He's alive," he confirmed.

Robbie's shoulders sagged. "Thank God. I didn't mean to

hurt him that badly."

"Well, you did hurt him, but you didn't kill him."

"He's still going to hate me when he wakes up."

"And why do we care about that? He threatened us with a gun."

"He was doing his job."

"Well, my job is to keep you and me alive, so I'll focus on that." Cyril looked around. "We don't know how long Vale and Russell are going to take, and I don't want to risk this guy attacking us if he wakes up. We should tie him up."

"With what? I don't know how to tie knots, and I don't walk around with ropes in my pockets."

Cyril was as lost as Robbie looked. "There has to be something in the van."

"Let's find it, then. I don't want the guy to be able to move when he opens his eyes."

Cyril nodded. The situation had gotten complicated fast, but he was glad that he and Robbie had managed to find a way to get out of the mess. They worked well together, which gave Cyril more hope that Robbie might want to stay with him long-term. Robbie would have to move out eventually, but if he was happy to work with Cyril, they could find a way to make it work.

First, they had a guard to tie up.

Vale and Russell moved in sync. Vale trusted Russell enough to know he didn't have to worry about what his friend was doing, so he focused on shooting the guard on his side.

The man went down without even noticing something was wrong. Blood spurted over the counter, darkening what appeared to be white marble.

Good luck getting the stains out of that.

Vale turned to West. The man was already moving, no

doubt rushing to his panic room so he could lock himself in. He was wearing pajama pants and a tank top, and his bare feet slid in the blood that was already spreading from the guard's head.

Vale knew where the panic room was. Rachel had explained that if West got in there, there would be no getting him out. Those things were built that way on purpose, which meant that if Vale wanted to kill West, he had to do it now or set the house on fire, which honestly didn't feel like such a bad idea. The place was ugly, anyway.

But instead of setting the house on fire, he shot a warning shot in front of Wes's head. The bullet embedded itself into the wall, and West jerked back, slipping on the blood and falling on his ass.

Vale glanced at Russell, who was staring at West. He tilted his head so that Russell knew to box West in, then walked around the counter, stepping over the dead body.

"It's been a while," he told West.

"You should be dead," West snarled.

"I should be, but the assassins you hired were sloppy. One is dead, by the way. I hope you didn't care too much about him."

"He couldn't do his job. He deserved to die."

"You know, we could've avoided all of this if you'd just left me alone," Vale pointed out. "Hiring me to kill the guy who was threatening to go to the authorities with proof that you killed your father wasn't a good idea. Didn't you think I would notice something was off?"

West glared, still sitting on the floor. Vale didn't care if he stayed there the entire conversation. It was over, anyway.

Cyril wouldn't be safe until West was gone, which meant that Vale needed to kill West. He didn't need West to monologue or beg. He just needed the guy to stop breathing.

"You shouldn't have come after me," he said.

"Wait! I can pay."

Vale shot him. West's body dropped, adding more blood to the puddle spreading on the floor. For a moment, everything was silent. The only sound Vale could hear was his and Russell's breathing.

"You think the other guards heard this?" Russell asked.

Vale glanced around the kitchen, but he couldn't hear or see anyone.

"I still have eyes on the guard in the servants' quarters, and he's watching TV, so you're good to leave," Rachel said in the earbud.

They were going to leave the poor guard a damn bad surprise. Vale felt a bit sorry for him since the guy had been hired to protect West, and West was dead, but he couldn't find it in himself to care much.

"Get me his phone," Rachel said. "Unlock it with his face or fingerprint or whatever he uses, then go into the settings and change that."

Russell took care of that while Vale kept an eye out. He couldn't believe this was finally over. He wasn't sure what West had thought he was doing by coming after him, but the man should have known things wouldn't work out. You didn't kill the assassins you hired to kill someone.

It just wasn't smart.

"Got everything," Russell said as he joined Vale.

"Let's go," Vale told him.

The sooner he was back with Cyril, the better he'd feel. He didn't like knowing that Cyril was out there, possibly in danger. He should have pushed for him to stay home, but Russell was right. Cyril would just have found a way to follow them, and then, he might've actually been in danger, and Vale wouldn't have known where to find him.

Russell clasped Cyril's shoulder. "Let's get you back to your man."

"Do you think we went a bit overboard with the tying thing?" Cyril asked as he and Robbie stared at the guard.

The only thing they'd found in the van that could be used to tie the guard had been several roles of adhesive tape, so that was what they'd used. Robbie had been especially enthusiastic about it, wrapping it around the guard until he looked like a weird spider had built a cocoon around him. The guard was still out, but even if he woke up, he wasn't going anywhere. Cyril was pretty sure that the only thing the man would be able to move was his eyes.

Robbie stared down at their work. "I don't know. Looks pretty good to me."

"He's definitely not going anywhere."

"That was the point."

"I know, but I feel sorry for him when he'll have to tear off all the tape. It's going to hurt like a bitch."

Robbie gave Cyril an incredulous glance. "Why do we care about that? He threatened us with a gun."

"Who threatened who with what?" Russell asked as he appeared from between the trees.

Vale was right behind him. Cyril forgot all about the guard and the hair on the guard's body as he rushed toward his boyfriend, needing to reassure himself that Vale was okay.

He threw himself into Vale's arms. Vale grinned at him, but it didn't last long because his gaze slid to the guard, who Robbie and Cyril had propped up against the van.

"What happened to him?" he asked, blinking.

"We went overboard with the tape," Cyril admitted.

"That's one way to put it. How many rolls did you use?"

"A few," Robbie said, grinning. "He should've known better than to threaten us with a gun. By the way, that gun is under the van, so we should probably pick it up before leaving."

Vale and Russell looked at each other. Russell started to laugh, and Robbie pushed him, glaring at him.

"What happened?" Vale asked Cyril while Russell got to his knees and reached under the van.

"He just appeared out of nowhere. He didn't hurt us. Robbie hit him on the head with a branch, and he hasn't woken up yet. He's not dead, but he probably has a concussion."

"That's not going to be great for him, but it's not a problem."

Cyril nodded because that was true. It wasn't their problem if the guy had a concussion or even if he died. It would be a pity because the man had only been doing his job, but it had been between him and Robbie and Cyril, and Cyril wasn't sorry.

"West?" he asked.

Vale pulled him closer and kissed the top of his head. "Gone. I have his phone, so Rachel will be able to check his accounts and the forum and ensure that the hit is taken down."

"Good." It was finally over. It was hard to believe, but Cyril couldn't wait to go back to a slightly more normal life. He doubted his life with Vale would ever be completely normal, but that wasn't what he needed or wanted.

He needed to be safe and for Vale to be, too. He needed them to be together.

That was pretty much it.

"You two did a good job," Russell said as he checked the gun before tucking it away. "Very enthusiastic," he told Robbie as he knocked their shoulders together. "I like your style."

Robbie's cheeks flushed. "I wasn't going to take shit from anyone else. West is really dead?"

"Very much so. He won't bother you or Vale ever again."

Robbie nodded and, to Cyril's surprise, leaned forward to

hug Russell.

Cyril looked away to give the two of them privacy. He didn't know what was happening between them, and it was none of his business, but he was curious, so maybe he would ask Robbie once they were home.

But the apartment wouldn't be Robbie's home for much longer. He'd probably stay a few more days just to ensure the coast was clear, but West was dead. Robbie didn't need to stay with Cyril and Vale anymore. Cyril was sure that all of them would be relieved because it had been a tight fit, but he'd miss Robbie.

He'd been a friend when Cyril hadn't had any friends. Well, he had Vale, and Russell and Rachel, but he considered them more family than friends. They would always be in his life because of Vale.

He couldn't say the same about Robbie.

"Are you sure you're okay?" Vale asked as he leaned closer, visibly worried.

What Cyril had been thinking had clearly been obvious in his expression. He didn't want his boyfriend to worry, especially with West gone. Vale had done too much worrying since the man had entered their life, and it was time for him to relax. Cyril wasn't sure that was something Vale was capable of doing, but they would find out.

Together.

"I'm just tired. It's been an eventful day."

Vale's gaze strayed to the guard. "I'd say. You did good, Cyril. I was afraid something would happen to you, and it did, but both you and Robbie made it out. I'm proud of you."

"Are you proud of me, too?" Russell asked.

Vale rolled his eyes. "Never."

Russell pouted as he guided Robbie toward the van. Robbie didn't hesitate before climbing in, showing everyone how eager he was to go home. Cyril felt the same, so he climbed in after him, leaving the guard to Vale and Russell. He didn't think they would kill him, but maybe it would be a good idea to call nine-one-one to get him help. That would complicate things since there were several dead bodies in the house, but as long as the authorities didn't know who'd called, maybe they could still help the guard.

He leaned closer as soon as Vale climbed into the driver's seat. "I think we should call for help," he suggested.

Vale groaned. "We can't."

"What if he has a concussion?"

Russell and Vale looked at each other. Russell appeared amused, and while Vale was huffing and puffing, Cyril knew that, eventually, he'd say yes.

He always said yes when Cyril asked for something. Cyril didn't usually take advantage of that, but this time, he might.

He didn't think Vale would mind.

EPILOGUE

Vale was going for a run, and this time, no one would try to kill him.

Hopefully.

Peter West was a thing of the past, but Vale was still slightly nervous as he got ready and kissed Cyril goodbye. He and Robbie were on the couch, watching whatever TV series they'd gotten into lately, but Vale could see something was up with his boyfriend. He wanted to ask, but he knew that Cyril would talk to him when he was ready. In the meantime, Vale would be here, ready for whatever came next.

He hoped they were done with near-death experiences. He'd had enough of them for a lifetime, and he didn't want Cyril to have to go through something like that again. Knowing their luck, someone else would come after them soon. Vale supposed that when it happened, he'd have to deal with it, but in the meantime, he wanted to forget all about his job and people wanting to kill him.

"I'll be back in about half an hour," he told Cyril. "I'm keeping it short today."

"We'll be here," Cyril promised as he pulled on the fraying sleeves of his sweater.

Vale leaned down again to kiss him. "Whatever's up with you, we can work on it together," he murmured.

"I'm fine."

"I didn't say you weren't." But he was clearly worried.

"I'm trying to watch this," Robbie bitched.

Vale glared at him, but there was no heat in it. He'd gotten used to having Robbie around. He wouldn't say he wanted Robbie to continue living with him and Cyril, but it hadn't been as uncomfortable as he'd expected it to be. All three of them had survived, and Robbie was finally free to do whatever he wanted. He didn't have to hide anymore. He could go back to his family, find another job, and hopefully, stay Cyril's friend through all of it.

Vale wasn't sure what he'd do if Robbie never wanted to see Cyril again because Cyril had latched onto him. The two of them had become friends while Robbie was staying at the apartment, and hopefully, his moving out wouldn't change that.

Vale left the two on the couch and stepped out of the apartment. He started moving toward the stairs, only to freeze when he noticed something on the doormat. For a moment, he just stared at it. It was a box, so nothing special, but the sight of it still made the hair on his head stand up. His fingers itched to check the cameras and see who'd left it there, but at the same time, he didn't want to focus on his phone when whoever had left this might still be in the area.

He couldn't stand there forever, staring at the box. He had to move, if anything, to make sure that Cyril was safe from whatever was in the box.

He listened to check in on Cyril, but the only thing he could hear was the TV. The box didn't seem to be a distraction. No one was screaming for help. No one was crying.

Yet.

Vale crouched next to the doormat and poked at the box. It wasn't heavy. It could be a body part, but he didn't think it was a bomb. Taking a deep breath, he pulled on the tape that kept it close.

He was still in one piece by the time he had the box open. He breathed easier as he leaned closer and peered into the box, but he was still wary.

The first thing he took out was a mug. The words *BFFs forever* were written on it in glittery pink. This was a very Russell thing to do, but there was a note inside the mug, and the handwriting on it didn't belong to Russell.

Vale was cautious as he picked up the note and read it.

I guess that the fact that I didn't kill you means we're BFFs forever now. You were lucky it was me and not someone else, although I heard you took care of the idiots who tried killing you. Good job, Roux. Enjoy the snacks I left you. I feel your boyfriend deserves them – he's adorable and way too good for you.

I'll see you when I see you.

Your BFF, Calypso.

Vale groaned and put the note back into the mug. He didn't trust Calypso, but he doubted she'd placed a bomb inside the box, so he continued poking at the contents. There was a box of chocolates, a bottle of wine, and a selection of snacks. Cyril was going to enjoy all of it thoroughly. Vale, on the other hand, wasn't sure he would be able to force himself to eat or drink anything, but he supposed he was going to try. There was no way Cyril wouldn't want him to enjoy this stuff with him.

With a sigh, he picked up the box and went back inside the apartment. Robbie and Cyril were where Vale had left them, and Cyril frowned as soon as he saw him.

"It's only been five minutes."

"Someone left a present on the doormat."

Robbie paused the show and turned to look at Vale. "Please tell me West had nothing to do with this."

"In a roundabout way, I guess he did. It's from Calypso."

Cyril and Robbie blinked. Even though they looked nothing alike, it made them look a bit like twins, which was kind of creepy, especially with Oscar nestled in between them with his bony tentacles extended on both their thighs.

"She sent snacks," Vale offered.

"Why would she do that? She's a professional assassin,"

Cyril said.

"She's trying to poison you," Robbie told him. "Or Vale. Probably Vale."

"You love me so much," Vale snarked.

"I wouldn't be here if I didn't. I'd have returned to my apartment and my family five seconds after West died."

Vale put the box on the coffee table. "Why haven't you?"

Robbie arched a brow. "Are you kicking me out?"

"I'm not. I'm just curious."

Robbie sighed. "I'm planning stuff. I know I have to move out, and it won't be long before I do. I'm just not sure if I want to return to my apartment. I definitely can't go back to my job."

"Why not? West is dead. Whoever's in charge of the company now might need an assistant."

Cyril sucked in a breath, catching Vale's attention. Something was happening there, and Vale didn't know what it was. He wouldn't find out until Cyril told him, but he might not want to do so in front of Robbie.

Was Robbie the problem? Did Cyril want him to leave sooner? Or maybe he didn't want Robbie to leave at all.

Vale knew a lot about his boyfriend's life. Because Cyril was a necromancer, a lot of people tended to stay away from him. That meant he didn't really have friends, and while he hadn't been a virgin when he'd met Vale, he'd also never been in a serious relationship before. He'd been a loner, and he still was, but now, he was a loner surrounded by people who loved him. He'd grown close to Robbie during the time Robbie had spent at the apartment, and Vale would call the two of them friends.

And maybe Cyril felt like he would lose his friend if Robbie moved out.

Cyril was sad. He'd known this would happen, and he'd told himself it would be better for everyone, including Robbie, but that didn't change the fact that he was disappointed.

Logically, there was no way for the three of them to continue living together. The apartment wasn't big enough, and they all deserved their privacy, especially Robbie. He'd been on the run for a while, hiding out and fearing for his life. He deserved to go back to everything he'd had to leave behind and feel safe again.

That didn't mean Cyril wasn't sad.

Of course Vale had noticed something was up. He arched a brow at Cyril, and Cyril realized he couldn't lie to his boyfriend. He didn't want to, and if he wanted to continue being friends with Robbie, he'd have to talk to him eventually. It wasn't a secret, so he might as well do it in front of Vale.

He cleared his throat. "There's no rush," he told Robbie. "You can stay here as long as you need."

Robbie laughed. "I'm pretty sure Vale disagrees with that."

"He doesn't. We both understand that you've been through hell and that you might need more time to feel safe."

Robbie reached out and squeezed Cyril's knee. "Thank you. It means a lot."

That was part one. Now, Cyril had to focus on part two. "I know you can't stay here forever because the apartment is too small, but I don't want us to lose the friendship we built. You were talking about a job and finding someone looking for an assistant, and well, maybe I have a solution. *I* need an assistant."

Robbie stared at Cyril with wide eyes. Cyril wasn't surprised at Robbie's reaction, but he *was* surprised at Vale's answer.

"I thought *I* was going to be your assistant," he complained.

Cyril blinked at him. "I can't imagine you'd be happy

doing that. I mean, you might initially, but it's pretty boring. You'd have to talk to families and things like that, and you're not exactly a people person."

"You're not wrong. It does sound boring, but I'd do it for you."

Cyril leaned forward. "And I love you for that. I know you're worried because you don't know what you'll do after you retire, but you'll find something."

"If I'm going to spend even more time with you two, you can't start making out with your boyfriend. I don't want to see that," Robbie said.

Cyril turned to him, afraid to hope. "What do you mean?"

"Exactly what I said. I'd like to talk about your offer and what it means, but I've enjoyed working with you."

"I thought that my ability freaked you out?"

Robbie cocked his head. "Are you trying to get me to change my mind already? You only just asked me to work with you."

"I don't want you to change your mind, but I also don't want you to be uncomfortable or feel that you have to do this just because Vale and I helped you."

"Oh, believe me, that's not why I'm taking the job. I'm grateful for everything the two of you did, and I'm still slightly uncomfortable with your ability, but I've seen what you can do. What better advertising than reanimating your own assistant, right?"

"I'd reanimate you a thousand times if necessary."

Robbie snorted. "Hopefully, you won't have to. I'm curious about how it works when you have to do it so many times, though. Maybe we can look into it."

Cyril grinned. Everything would be fine, after all. Robbie wanted to work with him, and Vale was safe. Russell had moved close by, and like Vale, he was talking about retiring. Maybe they could come up with a job together. No matter how much Vale bitched about Russell, they were best friends. They worked well together.

"I don't think I can ever thank the two of you enough for what you did for me," Robbie murmured. "But that's not why I want to do this. You're my friend, Cyril, and I don't want to lose that."

Cyril beamed and leaned over to hug Robbie. "You're my best friend."

"I thought that was Vale," Robbie murmured.

"He's my boyfriend, so it's different. I know that the way you came into my life was awful, but I'll never regret reanimating you."

Robbie snorted and leaned back. His eyes were suspiciously bright, as if he was about to cry. "You only did it because your boyfriend asked you to."

"Well, yes, but I couldn't imagine I'd find my best friend through a reanimation."

"Best friend, huh?"

Had him saying that been a mistake? Cyril didn't know how to behave when it came to people. He had more contact with dead bodies than living human beings, and sometimes, it was obvious in the way he talked to people. Maybe it would be too much for Robbie, after all. Still, Cyril had said it, so he might as well confirm it.

"If you want to be. As far as I'm concerned, you are."

Robbie smiled. "I'd like that."

"I feel like we should celebrate," Vale said as he reached into the box and took out a bottle of wine. "And Russell isn't even here. He's going to be so pissed when he finds out we celebrated without him. I'll have to send him pictures."

Cyril couldn't help but smile. No matter how many times Vale bitched about Russell, he knew that Vale cared about his best friend just like Cyril cared about his.

He could hardly believe it. Just a year ago, he'd been alone with only Oscar and sometimes his mother for company. Now, he had a boyfriend, a best friend, and two other friends who would do anything for him. People disliked the thought of death, but not Cyril. He'd always been friendly with death, but even more so now that it had brought him the people he cared the most about.

ABOUT THE AUTHOR

Catherine is the creator of several series, most of them paranormal, including the Whitedell Pride Series and the Gillham Pack Series. While she graduated in translation, she decided to go the writer's way because it was more fun to create her own stories and characters.

She's been living in Italy for more than twenty years, but she's a daughter of the North—Belgium to be precise—and she misses it so much that she's already planning to move back.

She loves pizza—probably too much—her son, her pets, and of course, books. She sneaks some reading time into her schedule every time she has five minutes free from writing, demands from her various pets and son, and lastly, housework.

Connect with her:

lievens.catherine@gmail.com
BookBub: https://www.bookbub.com/authors/catherine-lievens
Website: https://authorcatherinelievens.com/
Facebook: https://www.facebook.com/catherine.lievens.9
Facebook Group: https://www.facebook.com/groups/411788002341528/
Twitter: https://twitter.com/authorCLievens
Newsletter: http://eepurl.com/c-uvKn

www.ingramcontent.com/pod-product-compliance
Lightning Source LLC
Chambersburg PA
CBHW060625130626
46555CB00002B/660